## "Certainly You Remember Your Husband."

*Husband?* How could she not know her own name? Her own husband? "You can't be my— What are you doing?" Sarah gasped, struggling to move away.

"Refreshing your memory," Caleb said. "Is this familiar?" He slid one hand over her hip, while his arm pinned her against the mattress.

"No!" she cried out and moved his hand away. But somehow the touch *was* familiar.

He hesitated a moment, and she felt as if he were looking into her very soul, reading her deepest, darkest secrets. Secrets *she* didn't even know.

"Do you remember this?" he asked as his hand very slowly unbuttoned the top button of her shirt. His knuckles brushed the swell of her breast, but his dark gaze never left hers. Heat coursed through her.

She couldn't possibly desire a man she didn't even know. Could she?

Dear Reader,

This month, we begin HOLIDAY HONEYMOONS, a wonderful new cross-line continuity series written by two of your favorites—Merline Lovelace and Carole Buck. The series begins in October with Merline's *Halloween Honeymoon*. Then, once a month right through February, look for holiday love stories by Merline and Carole—in Desire for November, Intimate Moments for December, back to Desire in January and concluding in Intimate Moments for Valentine's Day. Sound confusing? It's not—we'll keep you posted as the series continues…and I personally guarantee that these books are keepers!

And there are other goodies in store for you. Don't miss the fun as Cathie Linz's delightful series THREE WEDDINGS AND A GIFT continues with *Seducing Hunter*. And Lass Small's MAN OF THE MONTH, *The Texas Blue Norther*, is simply scrumptious.

Those of you who want an *ultrasensuous* love story need look no further than *The Sex Test* by Patty Salier. She's part of our WOMEN TO WATCH program highlighting brand-new writers. Warning: this book is HOT!

Readers who can't get enough of cowboys shouldn't miss Anne Marie Winston's *Rancher's Baby*. And if you're partial to a classic amnesia story (as I certainly am!), be sure to read Barbara McCauley's delectable *Midnight Bride*.

And, as always, I'm here to listen to you—so don't be afraid to write and tell me your thoughts about Desire!

Until next month,

*Lucia Macro*

Senior Editor

---

# BARBARA McCAULEY
## MIDNIGHT BRIDE

SILHOUETTE *Desire®*

Published by Silhouette Books

America's Publisher of Contemporary Romance

SILHOUETTE BOOKS

ISBN 0-373-76028-0

MIDNIGHT BRIDE

**Books by Barbara McCauley**

Silhouette Desire

*Woman Tamer* #621
*Man from Cougar Pass* #698
*Her Kind of Man* #771
*Whitehorn's Woman* #803
*A Man Like Cade* #832
*Nightfire* #875
*\*Texas Heat* #917
*\*Texas Temptation* #948
*\*Texas Pride* #971
*Midnight Bride* #1028

*Hearts of Stone

---

## *BARBARA McCAULEY*

was born and raised in California and has spent a good portion of her life exploring the mountains, beaches and deserts so abundant there. The youngest of five children, she grew up in a small house, and her only chance for a moment alone was to sneak into the backyard with a book and quietly hide away.

With two children of her own now and a busy household, she still finds herself slipping away to enjoy a good novel. A daydreamer and incurable romantic, she says writing has fulfilled her most incredible dream of all: breathing life into the people in her mind and making them real. She has one loud and demanding Amazon parrot named Fred and a German shepherd named Max. When she can manage the time, she loves to sink her hands into fresh-turned soil and make things grow.

# One

The wolf paced, his massive black head slung low, his long, lean legs moving soundlessly over the cabin's hardwood floor. Flames crackled in the fireplace, reflecting in the animal's golden eyes. Eyes that were alert, watching. Waiting.

Caleb Hunter regarded the wolf's movements, tempted, for some strange reason, to follow suit. Outside the small cabin the wind howled and rain pummeled the A-frame roof. Inside, the scent of the storm mingled with smoke and filled the room.

But there was another scent. One that Caleb couldn't identify, but recognized instinctively.

Danger.

The wolf recognized it, too. He lifted his nose and sniffed, straightened his ears, then whined softly. Caleb set down the book he'd been reading.

"You, too, Wolf?" Caleb asked. Though hardly an original name, it suited the beast. Caleb had found the animal several months ago, half-dead, shortly after he'd come to the San Gabriel mountains outside of Los Angeles for a "much-needed rest and recuperation." Or so his superiors had said, shortly after he'd punched two of the bastards out.

Wolf whined again and stared at the cabin door. Lightning flashed, then thunder shook the walls. The animal's thick black fur lifted at his nape.

His own body tense, Caleb rose from his armchair by the fire and moved beside Wolf. The animal kept his gaze fixed on the door.

"I agree," Caleb said tightly. "What do you think we ought to do about it?"

A deep growl rumbled in Wolf's throat, then he padded to the door and stared at the knob.

"I thought you were going to say that," Caleb said with a sigh. He reached for the revolver he kept on the mantel, felt the weight of the cold steel on his palm. His grip tightened when the wind slammed against the doors and windows, then he slipped the weapon into the waistband of his jeans. He grabbed a flashlight, slipped on his heavy woolen jacket, then dropped a hat on his head.

Wolf bounded outside when Caleb opened the door. The wind sprayed the rain inside, and with a curse Caleb quickly closed the door behind him.

"Not a night fit for man or beast," he grumbled, pulling his jacket up tightly around his neck. Yet here they were, two misfits that belonged nowhere. To no one. Not even each other. Caleb may have pulled a hunter's bullet out of Wolf's shoulder and nursed him back to health, but they both knew the time here was temporary. But then, time anywhere was temporary, Caleb thought.

Even with the flashlight it was nearly impossible to see. Lightning lit the blackness, and through the pounding storm Caleb caught a glimpse of Wolf heading through the woods toward the creek bed.

Caleb followed. The drenched ground sucked at his boots. Water sluiced off the brim of his hat. His intellect told him that he was a complete fool to be out here, an observation he decidedly agreed with. No one ever came out this way, and certainly not in this weather. The closest neighbors, who lived in a cabin two miles away, were gone for the month, and the town of Pinewood was three miles away. It was only April, too early for campers.

But still, he felt it. In the wind, on the air. It was impossible to analyze, nothing that could be explained, but it was there nonetheless. Call it instinct, gut feeling, even extrasensory. He couldn't ignore it, he'd have been dead several times over if he had. It was the only thing he trusted blindly.

Something was out here that didn't belong. Something or someone.

An icy blast of wind struck him full force, sending a shiver clear through to his bones. Wolf's sharp bark several yards ahead brought Caleb's head up. "All right, boy, all right." He moved toward the sound. "I hear you."

He approached the edge of the creek. Normally the water was no more than a couple of feet deep and a gentle flow, but the violent storm had created a raging current. He heard Wolf's bark again, no more than a few feet away now. Caleb whistled shrilly, but the animal merely barked again, more insistently this time.

"It better not be a rabbit," Caleb muttered through clenched teeth, "or so help me you're stew."

Caleb swung the flashlight around, and the beam of light reflected off the beating rain. Wolf's bark turned to a growl. Caleb's fingers tightened on the flashlight. They weren't alone, and it sure wasn't any rabbit.

Caleb moved warily, closer to the edge of the creek; the barrel of his gun pressed into his waist. A chill slithered up his spine, but it had nothing to do with the cold. Wolf brushed against his leg, whined, then barked again. Jaw tight, Caleb turned, intending to move farther down the bank.

What he didn't intend was to fall over a tree limb.

The flashlight tumbled from his hands as he landed hard on his knees; mud oozed through his spread fingers. Barking, Wolf danced around him. *"Son of a—"*

He froze when the branch under his legs moved, then moaned.

"What the hell...?"

The dim glow of the flashlight a few feet away did little more than outline the figure he'd stumbled over. Caleb knelt beside the body and ran his hands over the limp form.

Female.

Lightning split the black sky, illuminating the woman lying on her back. She was slender, not too tall, and her clothes, a heavy sweater and thin skirt, clung to her like wet towels.

What in hell was a woman, alone, doing in the mountains at this time of year, in this kind of weather?

It was suicidal or downright idiotic. And while he hadn't the patience for either reason, he certainly couldn't leave her here.

As if to punctuate his thought, lightning and thunder struck simultaneously. He watched the woman's eyes fly open, and she attempted to sit. The weight of the mud held her like flypaper. He reached for the flashlight and tucked it under his arm, then took hold of her shoulders and pulled her up.

*"What are you doing out here?"* he yelled over the pounding rain.

Her answer was no more than a whimper. He tightened his grip on her and shook her lightly. *"Are you hurt?"*

Her hair hung like wet strings across her face. She blinked several times, then lifted her gaze to him. Her eyes widened in horror.

*"No-o-o-o!"*

She swung a fist at him and struck him on the chin, though the mud covering her hand carried more weight behind it than her punch. She struggled weakly, frantic to get away, but hadn't the strength of a wet leaf.

"Calm down," Caleb shouted, then lifted her in his arms and stood. He felt her resistance, heard her cry of protest. The fool woman didn't even *want* to be rescued, he thought with annoyance.

Even soaking wet, she weighed no more than a feather. He balanced the flashlight under his arm and started back toward the cabin, bending his head down when a stiff gust of wind pelted them. The woman trembled in his arms and huddled against him, muttering incoherently. Her shivering was a good sign. If hypothermia had taken hold, she would have shown no reaction to the cold. He pulled her closer to him, trying to shield her drenched body, but there was little he could do in a storm this violent.

Wolf ran ahead, barking sharply if Caleb fell too far behind. By the time they reached the cabin, the temperature had dropped and the rain had turned to sleet.

"You're one lucky lady," he muttered roughly as he yanked open the front door. "A few more minutes out in that and you would have been a Popsicle."

As if understanding his words, the woman groaned, a soft, low sound of anguish. He cradled her against him and moved inside the cabin, then kicked the door shut after Wolf ran inside. Caleb moved straight to the fire and sat on the stone hearth, shifting his cargo so her head lay back against his arm.

"Well, now," he said, taking the woman's chin in his hand, "let's have a look at you."

She was young, in her twenties, he guessed. Her bone structure was small, and she had a fragile quality about her. Mud streaked her high cheeks and forehead, and her hair lay plastered in flat curls against her pale skin. He saw blood on his fingers and gently turned her head until he saw the gash behind her left ear.

"Damn," he muttered. "Looks like we're going to have to get you to a doctor, darlin'."

"No."

The word was barely audible. Surprised, Caleb glanced back to her face. Her eyes fluttered open. They were blue...a soft, baby blue, rimmed by dark, thick lashes. For one split second, in the space between heartbeats, Caleb felt as if the floor had dropped out beneath him. Stunned, he quickly shook the feeling off.

"No doctor," she said hoarsely, staring at him through a glaze of pain. She lifted one hand and wrapped her slender fingers around the lapel of his jacket. "No doctor, no police." Shivering, she squeezed her eyes shut. "They'll find me...please... don't let them find me...*please*...no one..."

"Who?" Caleb asked. "Who will find you?"

"Please." Her whispered plea faded, but the urgency in her voice and bottomless eyes echoed in Caleb's mind. Her head rolled back, and her hand slipped from his jacket.

He ran his hands under her sweater and down her skirt; she recoiled instinctively at the intimate intrusion. No ID, no purse or wallet, he noted. A chain around her neck sparkled in the firelight. Caleb lifted the necklace and fingered the letters engraved in gold: Sarah.

Had someone sent her? he wondered. He'd been careful, but it was possible they'd managed to find him here after six months. He knew that sooner or later they would make an attempt to get to him, but would they send a woman in after him, especially one so young and obviously inexperienced? It was hard to imagine, which made him all the more suspicious.

Thunder shook the walls again. She'd have her wish tonight, anyway, he thought with a frown. He had no phone to call anyone, and even if he had, no one was getting in or out on the main road now.

He looked at the woman in his arms. *Sarah.*

"Well, Sarah, darlin', looks like you're staying here with Wolf and me for now." He sighed, then gathered her close and stood. "Let's say we get you out of those wet things, shall we?"

* * *

A marching band pounded in her head. The trumpets wailed and the trombones blared. She tried to move, but the effort set off the drum section. *Lie still,* she told herself, not understanding the origin of her pain, but fully understanding the sensation. Breath held, she waited until the first sharp wave of agony passed through her.

The beating in her head slowed and settled into a dull ache. The marching band moved on, replaced by silence. No, not quite silence, she decided. She heard the drumming of rain now, the howl of wind. And breathing. The sound of deep, steady breaths.

Whose breathing?

She fought back the unreasonable panic that rose suddenly in her. *Stay calm,* she repeated over and over until her heart slowed its thunderous pace. Logic told her that control was important, composure essential. She counted to ten, willing her nerves to be still.

She lay on her back, on a soft mattress; a pillow cradled her head. She moved her fingers, felt the smooth warmth of the blanket covering her. *I'm in a bed,* she realized, but knew it wasn't her own.

The scent of wood smoke seemed to surround her. Camping? The mountains? Slowly, cautiously, she opened her eyes.

It was like looking through a lens out of focus. There were shapes and color, but everything was blurred. She blinked several times, waiting for the images to take form.

The ceiling was open beam. Dark, heavy boards, rough-hewn. The walls were logs. A cabin? She glanced to her left. A small lamp glowed on a pine dresser, filling the room with a soft yellow light. Rain beat against a window over the dresser. It was dark out. She shivered involuntarily and closed her eyes again, not understanding her sudden and intense fear. She waited, letting the emotion pass.

She heard the breathing again. Deep, slow. Steady. She opened her eyes and glanced to the right.

A man. Sitting in a rocker beside the bed. His head hung forward, and she couldn't see his face. But his hair was black as the night, his hands large, his chest and shoulders broad. He wore a blue flannel shirt and faded jeans. He was sound asleep.

She tried to sit, but the movement was like swinging a hammer inside her head. She drew in a breath, waiting for the pain to subside.

A strange bed. A strange place. A strange man.

She opened her eyes again, and this time he was staring right at her. Her breath caught.

Shadows hid half of his face, giving the illusion of a mask. A phantom. He said nothing, just looked at her, his expression as dark as his hair. She felt as if she'd stepped into a stage play and he would rip the mask away to reveal his horrible disfigurement. A scream bubbled deep in her throat, but she hadn't the strength to release it. Her heart raced as he stood and moved closer.

Other than a scar over his left eyebrow, there was no disfigurement, she realized with intense relief. In fact, he was rather good-looking, in a rugged, masculine way. A face that appealed not on an aesthetic level, but a primitive one.

He stood over her, and she lifted her gaze to his. He was tall, much too tall, she decided, hating the way he towered over her.

"How's your head?" he asked.

His voice was deep, husky. She'd heard it somewhere before, but it hurt too much to try to think of where. "Who—"

Her throat felt like sandpaper. The bed dipped low as the man sat beside her and slipped his hand behind her neck. He carefully lifted her head and offered her a drink of water from a glass on the nightstand. The cool liquid eased the tightness in her throat.

"Who are you?" she asked hoarsely. The room was in focus now, and the persistent throb in her head quieted. "Where am I?"

"Why, Sarah, darlin'," the man said, "after all we've meant to each other, you don't remember me?"

Confused, she stared at the man. Was that sarcasm she heard in his voice? "Why... why did you call me Sarah?"

He lifted one dark brow. "What should I call you?"

She opened her mouth, but no sound came out.

*What should I call you?*

The pounding in her head increased. Her name.

*What was her name?*

"I—I don't know," she said weakly.

He narrowed his eyes. "You don't remember your name?"

She closed her eyes against the encroaching pain. "No."

The weight on the bed shifted, and her eyes flew open again as the man climbed under the covers beside her.

That's when she realized what she was wearing. An oversize white cotton shirt with the sleeves rolled up and a pair of thermal underwear.

"What are you doing?" she gasped, struggling to move away. The man draped an arm around her waist and held her still.

"Refreshing your memory," he said. "Is this familiar?"

He slid a hand over her hip.

"No!" she cried out and moved his hand away. But somehow, the touch *was* familiar. Yet not.

He raised himself on one elbow and stared down at her. "It's me, Sarah. Caleb. Certainly you remember your husband."

Her eyes widened. *Husband?*

"You can't be my— I can't be your—"

She bit her lip. How could she not know her own name? Her own husband?

"That's not possible," she whispered. "I—I don't remember you...or us..."

He hesitated a moment, and she felt as if he were looking into her very soul, reading her deepest, darkest secrets. Secrets *she* didn't even know.

"Do you remember this?" he asked, and ran his hand up her arm, then traced her collarbone with his fingers. Her heart began to race, and her breathing came in short, quick gasps. "Or maybe you remember this?"

His hand dropped lower, very slowly unbuttoning the top button of the shirt she wore. His knuckles brushed the swell of her breast, but his dark gaze never left hers. Her skin tightened, her body came alive with a mind all of its own. Heat coursed through her, a mixture of embarrassment and—what? Desire?

No, she didn't remember him, and this most certainly was *not* familiar. She couldn't speak, all she could do was shake her head.

He stopped. So did her breathing. He watched her for a long moment, then refastened the button and inched away. Reluctantly, she thought.

"I don't understand," she muttered. "What's happened to me?"

"You hit your head," he said. "You were... out in the storm and fell."

The storm. She looked toward the window, stared at the rain beating against the panes...

*She was falling... falling. River. Cold.*

She sat up quickly, then squeezed her eyes shut and gasped at the pain that shot through her head.

"Lie back," the man—Caleb—said. "Here, take these." He reached toward the nightstand, then pressed something into her mouth. Aspirin. His touch was gentle, and she didn't resist when he held the glass to her lips. She swallowed, coughing as the tablets went down her throat.

"Get some rest now." Caleb slipped out from under the covers. She almost reached for him, felt frightened and cold with him gone. She clutched the blankets to her instead, wishing the blasted pounding in her head would stop.

And as the medication slowly took effect, she slipped into blessed sleep with a strange image. Her bare skin, wet and slick, against Caleb's.

Caleb stared out the kitchen window, listening to the coffee percolate as the sky transformed from inky black to dusty gray. Rain fell steadily, alternating between hail and sleet, though not with the intensity of the night before. The thunder had moved north and was no more than an occasional distant rumble. He knew from experience the storm wasn't finished just yet. Before the day was through, there would undoubtedly be another assault.

And before the day was through, he also intended to have some answers.

*Sarah.* He glanced at the wall separating the kitchen from the bedroom. He wasn't even sure that was her name, but for now it would have to do.

A scratch at the back door caught Caleb's attention, and he let a soggy Wolf inside. The animal gave himself a shake, then padded across the kitchen into the living room. Caleb frowned at the paw prints on the hardwood floor. They had an understanding, he and Wolf. Caleb kept his food bowl filled, and the animal in turn kept unwanted visitors, human or otherwise, at bay.

Until last night.

With a sigh, he poured himself a cup of coffee, then sat at the kitchen table and ran a hand over the beginning stubble of a beard. So what did he know about his midnight intruder? She was probably in her mid-twenties, approximately five foot three, maybe 110 pounds dripping wet, shoulder-length pale blond hair. Blue eyes. He remembered his initial reaction to those eyes, then frowned and continued his evaluation. Identifying marks: one small scar on her inside right elbow, approximately two and a half centimeters, and a small, heart-shaped mole on her left thigh. Caleb smiled. A very nicely shaped thigh at that, but he doubted that his mystery woman would appreciate that opinion.

She hadn't been dressed for a hike in the mountains, carried no identification, wore no wedding band. Her hands and legs were badly scratched, and she had a minor laceration behind her left ear.

And no memory.

He leaned back in his chair and took a swallow of the strong coffee. She was either telling the truth about not knowing who she was or was one hell of a good liar. He'd made up the story about being her husband and climbed into bed with her just to rattle her. Instead, *he'd* been the one rattled. The innocence that had shimmered from her was like a punch in the gut.

True, he'd been without female companionship for a long time, but he'd never remembered any woman being so soft, so delicate, or smelling so sweet. No woman had ever looked at him with such complete trust. Or made him feel like such a complete heel. He'd spent the rest of the night on the couch, alternating between sleep and listening for any sounds from the bedroom, but there'd been nothing.

If she hadn't been sent here to find him, then who the hell was she? Beautiful women didn't just fall out of the sky. He was more than a mile in from the main road, and the closest rental cabin was more than two miles away. She couldn't have walked. Not in this storm. She had to have a car somewhere. Or be with someone who had a car.

*Please don't let them find me,* she'd said.

Don't let *who* find her? And why had she begged him not to call the police or a doctor? Caleb narrowed his eyes as he stared at the steam rising from his coffee. If he was being set up, she was doing one hell of a job.

Which gave him all the more reason not to trust her.

He shoved his cup aside. He'd go back down to the creek later when the storm eased and check out the area. But right now he had lots of questions and no patience. It was time for Sleeping Beauty to wake up. He rose and headed for the bedroom.

Her scream stopped him halfway.

# Two

Sarah threw the covers over her head and attempted to burrow herself into the bed. When she felt the mattress dip, she screamed again.

"Sarah!" Strong, large hands grabbed her shoulders. "What's the matter?"

"An animal!" She buried herself as deeply under the blankets as possible. "There's a wild animal in your bedroom!"

The hands stilled, then she heard a deep chuckle. "It's only Wolf."

"A wolf!" She huddled closer to Caleb. "Shoot it!"

Caleb tugged at the blankets. "Come out from under there."

*And be eaten alive? Was he crazy?* She hugged the covers tighter.

Caleb yanked the covers off.

Sarah squeezed her eyes shut. When the beast barked, she hollered and launched herself at Caleb, which sent them both sprawling on the floor. Caleb landed on his back, with Sarah on top of him.

"Sarah!" He rolled her underneath him. "For God's sake, will you stop!"

At the sound of a deep growl inches away from her ear, Sarah went completely still. Her heart stopped, she couldn't breathe. And with Caleb's body on top of hers, she couldn't move. Slowly she opened her eyes.

Golden wolf eyes stared back.

With a whimper, Sarah turned her head. The cold hardwood floor pressed against her cheek. Caleb's hands circled her wrists and held them firmly to her sides. She felt herself go limp, heard the animal bark again, but it sounded far away this time, as if she were in a metal drum...

*Don't let her get away, dammit! Kill her if you have to, but don't let her get away!*

*Kill her... kill her... kill her...*

"Sarah."

She heard someone calling gently. *Sarah?* Was that her name? The man, Caleb, had told her it was. He called to her again, and her eyelids fluttered open.

"Sarah," he said again, "this is Wolf. He won't hurt you."

She turned her head slowly toward the animal. It cocked its massive black head as it stared down curiously at her. Panic washed through her, and she struggled to free her arms.

"He won't hurt you," Caleb reassured her, holding her tightly. "He thinks we're playing, and he wants to join in. He's just a big baby."

"Playing?" Sarah croaked out. *"Big baby?"*

Caleb grinned down at her. "Sure. He's hardly more than a pup."

"A *pup?*" Sarah eyed the wolf warily. Its tongue hung sideways from its huge jaw, and its tail wagged furiously. "That's like saying Moby Dick was a fish."

With a bark, the beast lunged at her. Sarah's scream lodged in her throat as a long, wet tongue washed over her cheek.

"Wolf!" Caleb said sternly. "Back!"

Reluctantly the animal backed up and sat on his haunches.

Though it was only seconds, it seemed like hours until Sarah could breathe again. Concern filled Caleb's eyes as he looked down at her. "You okay?"

She nodded slowly, then drew in a calming breath.

And just as she felt herself relax, Sarah became fully aware of Caleb's body stretched over her own. Her senses sharpened with razor precision. Every hard muscle of his lower body pressed intimately against her. His legs against hers, his thighs, the bulge of his manhood. A bulge that seemed to suddenly be growing....

Her eyes widened as she stared up at him. He gazed at her with a dark intensity that made her heart race and her stomach turn inside out. Heat radiated from his skin, burning through fabric and skin...down to her very soul. She caught the scent of coffee and soap, felt the rough texture of his callused hands on her wrists.

*Her husband?*

Was it truly possible she could forget a man like this? A man who turned her brain to mush and set her insides on fire? She searched the rugged lines of his face, the strong set of his jaw, the hard, sensuous mouth.

Her skin tightened, and a warm, pleasurable flush filled her. The cotton shirt she wore rubbed almost painfully against the hardened nipples of her breasts, and she became exceedingly aware of her nakedness underneath. She wanted him to touch her, to feel his skin on hers, and that realization brought a hot blush to her cheeks.

*Her husband?*

Could it really be? Could a woman such as herself possibly be married to a man like this? Yet that thought unto itself confused her. She hadn't any idea what *kind* of woman she was.

He watched her; she saw the same primitive fierceness in his eyes that she'd seen in the wolf. She thought to use the same command on him that he'd used on the animal, but somehow she doubted that yelling *back* at the man would have any effect.

"Caleb," she whispered, "let me up."

He didn't move.

A pulse throbbed deep in her throat, and a wild excitement swirled low in her belly. She looked at Caleb, felt the current of tension course from his body into hers. An image flashed through her mind; sensations and sounds, but no definition. The feel of his hands on her wet, bare skin... water... a warm fire.

She wasn't ready for this—this intimacy. He was a stranger to her. A face with no memories, only feelings. Feelings that frightened her.

"Please," she said softly, then wondered herself if it was *please touch me,* or *please don't.*

He loosened his hold on her, then slowly rose, pulling her with him and setting her on the edge of the bed. The movement made her head swim and reminded her that someone with a tiny hammer was busy inside her head.

"You all right?"

She nodded, then winced at the pain the gesture cost her.

He sat beside her. "Here, let me take a look at that."

She bent her head. "What happened to me?"

"You hit your head," he said and lifted the bandage he'd applied. "Probably on a rock, or rocks, based on the number of bruises and scratches all over your body."

She felt every one of them. She ached from one end of her body to the other. "But *how* did it happen?"

"I don't know."

"I was outside alone? In a storm?"

He hesitated, then reapplied the bandage. His fingers brushed her neck as he pulled away, and she couldn't stop the shiver that ran along her spine.

When he didn't answer, she looked up at him. He stared at her, his mouth hard, his eyes narrowed. There was no emotion there, and he looked at her now as if *she* were a stranger. One not to be trusted.

A different shiver, this time one of fear, crept through her. She tightened her hold on the blankets, trying to still the trembling in her hands. Slowly she lifted her gaze to his. "Did you... do this... to me?"

Surprise clearly registered on his face, then exasperation. "No, Sarah, I didn't do this to you."

She believed him. She had no idea why she should, but she did. She let out the breath she'd been holding. "But you don't know what happened?"

He shook his head, then ran a hand through his thick black hair. She stared at his large hands, then looked at her own.

"If we're married," she said carefully, "where are our rings?"

He said nothing.

She went still, then whispered, "We aren't married, are we?"

"No."

The strangest mixture of relief and disappointment filled her.

And fear.

She closed her eyes and started to shake. What was happening? She had no idea where she was or even *who* she was. She was in the bed of a man she didn't know, and she looked and felt as if she'd been the piñata at a child's party.

The man inside her head with a hammer switched to a chainsaw. She opened her eyes again and, through a haze of pain, focused on the stranger sitting beside her. He watched her as if *he* were the one confused, as if *he* were suspicious of her.

"Do you even know me?" she asked.

"No."

*No?* She drew in a slow breath and pulled the covers closer. He'd said they were married. He'd even climbed into bed with her. *That* she certainly remembered. Distinctly. Had he thought to take advantage of her in her weakened state? To make her believe they were husband and wife so she wouldn't fight him if he—

No. She didn't believe that. He'd had every opportunity if he'd wanted to use her like that. He still did. She was weak as a kitten. He was a big, strong man.

It would be impossible to stop him if he had ill intentions toward her. And besides, a man with Caleb's looks didn't need to trick any woman into his bed. They'd have to take a number and stand in line. A long line.

"Why... why did you lie to me?" she asked quietly.

His eyes narrowed, and the lines beside his mouth deepened. Rain battered the roof; wind whipped the branches against the window; but the silence between them closed around them like a vise. And that look was there again, in his dark eyes, in the lines between his brows. And then she realized.

*He* was the one who didn't trust *her*.

"You were testing me, weren't you?" she asked. "You thought I was lying when I told you I don't know who I am."

He stood then and looked down at her. She not only felt weak as a kitten, she suddenly felt as small as one, too. He was so tall, six-three at least, she guessed. She'd felt that body against her own, every rock-hard muscle. Everything about the man was dark and dangerous.

And wildly, incredibly exciting.

"Why, Caleb?" she asked again. "Or is that really your name?"

He nodded slowly. "It is. Caleb Hunter."

*Hunter.* How appropriate, she thought. And she was the prey. Like a cornered, frightened bird, her heart raced, but she was unable to move, even as he sat back down beside her.

"And my name? Did you make that up?"

He reached toward her, hesitating when she shrank back, then slipped his hand under the collar of her shirt. Her breath held as his fingers skimmed her collarbone. She felt him gently tug on a chain around her neck she hadn't realized she wore.

"You came with an ID tag," he said with a crooked smile.

Her hand brushed his as she reached up to touch the necklace. His skin was hot and rough, hers cool and smooth, a blaring reminder of his masculinity against her femininity. A woman alone, with a man she didn't know.

She held his gaze as he pulled away, then glanced down at the chain. *Sarah.* A sweeping script of gold letters. She ran her fingers over each letter, trying desperately to remember something, *anything*. But as before, the attempt only intensified the pounding in her head.

The room began to spin. She swayed slightly, then felt Caleb's hands on her shoulders, guiding her backward. The pillow cushioned her head, and her pain eased.

"You need to rest," he said, and started to rise.

"No!" She laid her hand on his arm. "I have to know something. Whatever you can tell me."

With a sigh, Caleb sat back down. "It was almost midnight. Wolf was unusually restless, agitated, as if he knew there was something wrong. I followed him down to the creek, which is more like a river right now, and I stumbled over you."

Stunned, Sarah looked at the animal, who had settled down contentedly beside the bed. "I was alone? In the middle of the night, in a storm?"

He nodded. "Not exactly a healthy pastime."

She struggled to keep her mind clear, to try to comprehend even a little of what Caleb told her. "Why didn't you take me to the hospital? Or call the police?"

He shook his head. "The roads weren't passable last night."

"And now?"

He stared at her for a long time, then rose and walked to the window. Rain streaked the glass, and a sudden flash of lightning backlit Caleb's tall form. Thunder rumbled close by.

"Last night," he said, turning to face her, "after I got you back to the cabin, you gained consciousness for a few moments. You pleaded with me not to call anyone."

"*I* pleaded with you? Why would I do that?"

"That's what I would like to know."

There it was again, she thought with confusion. The mistrust. But why? If he truly didn't know her, or she him, why would he be suspicious? He moved toward her again, arms at his sides, carefully watching her face.

"You begged me not to let them find you," he said, standing beside the bed.

"Them?" She pressed her fingers to her temple and rubbed at the stabbing pain that sliced through her head. "Who?"

"I was hoping you might be able to tell me that," he said without emotion. "You said, 'no doctor, no police, don't let them find me.' You also had no ID on you."

She'd told him not to call anyone? That made no sense at all. "Is that why you don't trust me, why you don't believe me? You think I'm an escaped criminal and I'm on the run?" she asked incredulously.

"You could be anyone, darlin'," Caleb said dryly. "But one thing is clear. You were definitely on the run. From something, or somebody."

If she'd had the strength she would have laughed. *On the run.* Why would someone like her be running from anyone? Ridiculous. Except—she closed her eyes as the pain became nearly unbearable—she didn't *know* what she was like.

A moment passed, then she felt Caleb lift her head and press two aspirin into her mouth. She didn't want them, she wanted her head to be clear so she could think.

But what good would it do to fight him? He was right; she did need to rest. She could think later, sort it out. Surely by the time she woke up, she would have her memory back, and she could call someone to come get her. Just an hour or two, then the pieces would fall in place.

*You could be anyone.* Caleb's words sent a chill up her spine.

She swallowed when he held the water glass to her lips. His hands were gentle as he laid her head back down. Her lids were heavy, but she forced them open.

"Hey, Caleb," she murmured as he turned to leave.

He looked back at her. "Yeah?"

"I think I liked it better when we were married."

Caleb finished unloading the groceries he'd picked up in town, then moved into the living room. The fire he'd started almost two hours before was nearly gone, and a chill had settled into the cabin. Sparks flew when he threw three more logs into the fireplace, and new flames crackled to life.

After Sarah had fallen back asleep, there'd been a break in the storm and he'd decided to drive into town while the roads were passable. He'd made some inquiries—whether there'd been any accidents on the mountain during the storm or if any strangers had been in—but no one had seen or heard anything unusual. He'd also stopped by the sheriff's for a casual chat, but again, nothing. After buying a few things, he'd hurried back to the cabin just in time for the sky to open up again and unleash the current downpour. Wolf, who'd been posted outside Sarah's door while he'd been gone, had taken off for parts unknown, mindless of the weather.

Caleb threw another log on the fire and brushed his hands off on his jeans. He wasn't expecting snow, but with the temperature dropping steadily over the past couple of hours, no doubt there'd be a coat of ice outside tonight thick enough to skate on. He frowned as he realized it might be difficult getting out again for a day or two.

Which also meant it would be difficult getting in.

*Please don't let them find me.*

Caleb narrowed his eyes and stared into the dancing flames. Sarah's words and the desperate tone in her voice played over and over in his mind. She'd been nearly unconscious when he'd brought her in from the storm. Why would he give credence to anything a half-drowned, incoherent female said? Especially one who'd had a knock on the head. For all he knew, she might have meant the little green men with four eyes and antenna hair.

He knew a lot about paranoia. It ran deep, made a person suspicious of everyone from the mailman to little girls selling cookies.

And most especially, to women who washed up on the bank of a creek in the middle of the night—right outside the door of a high-level federal government agent, whom half the agency wanted to find and reinstate in service, and the other half wanted to kill.

He certainly wouldn't put it past the agency to sink to a stunt like this. Sending a female operative to find him. Not to bring him back, of course. Even though it had been six months, they knew only too well that no one could bring him back until he was damn good and ready. If she was an agent, her duty would be to assess the situation and report back, nothing more.

He smiled slowly. Between climbing into bed with her, then rolling on the floor with her this morning, she'd certainly have plenty to report. Just thinking about those long legs and how incredibly soft her body had been underneath his brought an instantaneous tightening in his lower regions. And those eyes of hers. Lord help any man who fell into those baby blues.

With a sigh, he picked up the fireplace poker and stabbed at the logs. He just couldn't believe that the woman he'd pulled out of mud and water in near freezing temperature worked with the government. He'd always had an uncanny ability to spot another operative, and he didn't want to believe that the agency would stoop that low, or jeopardize the life of an agent that way.

But hadn't that kind of thinking nearly killed him seven months ago?

It *had* killed Tom and his wife, Jenny. Agents in Caleb's department rarely married or had families. They didn't even have friends. It was too risky. Not only because the work was dangerous, but the threat of retaliation and blackmail against loved ones was too great. And once an agent was in this highly specialized department, they didn't get out. If you married, your spouse took the same risks as you. Tom and Jenny had known that and taken that risk. They hadn't even seen their first anniversary.

Caleb's hand tightened around the poker as he stared into the flames. He still woke up at night with the sound of the explosion, still heard Jenny's screams....

That operation had been one massive screwup. After he'd gotten out of the hospital, Caleb had found every man responsible and had graphically demonstrated his anger. If it hadn't been for Mike, and the man's rank in the department, Caleb would be in the brig right now, instead of on a leave of absence.

Mike Townsend was the only person Caleb would ever trust again. The only man he truly called friend. They'd entered the agency at the same time fourteen years ago and had both risen quickly, with Mike choosing command positions and Caleb preferring the hands-on assignments. They'd been to hell and back together, and each of them had saved the other's life. More than once.

That's why, when he'd gone to town earlier, he'd called Mike, who had sworn he hadn't sent an agent in. But Caleb knew that didn't rule out the possibility someone else in the department had without Mike's knowledge. And there was always the possibility, though remote, that she was from another department, or even less remote, from another government. Caleb had information that men—or women—would kill for. If they'd found out he was here, they might try to get at him through a woman.

He would know soon enough. He'd mailed the water glass she'd drunk from to Mike. Her fingerprints would reveal the true identity of his mystery woman.

"Caleb?"

He turned sharply at the unexpected sound, the poker raised and ready to strike. She stared at him from the bedroom doorway, eyes wide, one hand clutching the top of the shirt she wore. With a curse he slowly lowered the weapon.

Sarah's first impulse was to bolt back into the bedroom and lock the door, but her feet wouldn't move. She swallowed the lump in her throat and stood at the door. "I—I'm sorry. I didn't mean to sneak up on you."

"You shouldn't be up," he said tightly.

"I'm feeling much better."

Except for the light from the fire, darkness cloaked the room. Shadows flickered on Caleb's face. He looked fierce and powerful. Dangerous. His dark gaze fell on her.

Why was he staring at her like that? she wondered. Not just staring *at* her, but *into* her. As if he knew things she didn't. She almost laughed at the irony of that, considering she knew *nothing* about herself. She felt her breath release as he set the poker back into its holder.

"I didn't mean to intrude." She took a hesitant step into the room. "I thought I might use your phone."

He raised one brow. "And call whom?"

"The police, to start. Maybe someone has filed a missing person's report or they found my car."

He moved beside her. "I just got back from town, Sarah. There's been no report made, no car found."

"That—that's not possible," she whispered.

"Apparently it is."

The room began to spin. She reached back toward the doorway, but suddenly found herself off the ground and in Caleb's arms.

"I'm fine," she protested. "Really."

He carried her to the fire and set her on the seat of the brick hearth. "Right. And I'm Don Quixote."

She touched her trembling fingers to her temple. "No. You're much too dark and handsome. I'd say more like Brontë's Heathcliff."

Sarah nearly gasped at the audacity of her words. *My God, did I really say that?* Heat rushed to her cheeks as she looked up at Caleb.

He stood over her, thumbs hooked in the front loops of his jeans. Amusement lit his eyes; firelight danced in his black hair. She wanted the floor to open up and swallow her whole. Frantically she searched her aching brain, trying to think of a retraction. *Oh, sure,* she thought irritably, *now I can't think of a thing to say.*

"How's your head?" he asked.

"I think the construction crew is taking a break right now." She caught a flash of straight white teeth just before he sat down next to her.

"Let me take a look at it."

"No, really, it's fine."

But he was already reaching for her, and there was nothing she could do, outside of jumping into the fire. When his thigh brushed hers, she nearly did that.

"Turn around." He took hold of her shoulders and turned her body until her back was to him. It was impossible to stop the shiver that raced up her spine as he swept her hair aside.

"This might hurt."

It didn't. Quite the opposite. A delicious tingling sensation skimmed over her head and neck, spreading down her shoulders. When he tugged the bandage off, the tingling only intensified.

He angled her head toward the light of the fire. The heat from the flames burned through the cotton of her shirt and thermal underwear, but the whisper of Caleb's breath on her neck was like a long, slow sip of warm brandy. She closed her eyes and, in spite of herself, felt herself relax as his fingers roamed the base of her neck.

He carried the scent of the storm on his skin, she thought languidly, and something else, something even more potent, more enticing. *His* scent. A mixture of soap and pine and untamed masculinity. Her pulse tripped, then bolted.

"That's strange," he said thoughtfully.

She held back another shiver as his fingers combed through her hair. "What?"

"Unusual."

"What?"

"Your hair."

"What about my hair?"

"It's natural."

It took a moment for his words to sink in. With a cluck of annoyance, she pulled away and turned to face him. "I've misplaced an entire life, nearly died, and you're making jokes."

"It's not a joke. Your hair *is* natural."

He wanted to tell her that it was soft, too. Like spun silk. His hands ached to lose themselves in those golden strands. When he saw tears glisten in her eyes, he cursed his lust and let his hands fall to his sides.

"I looked in the mirror in the bathroom," she whispered raggedly. "A stranger stared back at me. Have you any idea what that's like?"

*More than you could possibly know,* he thought.

"Caleb." She lifted her gaze to his. "I want you to take me into town, to the sheriff."

He wanted to agree with her. For her sake, as well as his. There had to be someone looking for her—family or friends. And he sure as hell didn't need an angry husband breaking his door down. Whatever trouble she'd gotten into was her problem, not his. It made no sense for her to stay here. No sense at all.

But he couldn't let go of the desperation in her voice and the fear in her eyes when he'd found her. If it had been an act, it had been a damn good one. But if it wasn't, then someone had tried to kill her, and that someone might try again.

"All right." He stood and looked down at her. "Let's say I take you in. Then what?"

Her brow furrowed. "I—I don't understand."

"As of one hour ago there was no missing person's report or any car found. My closest neighbors, a German family named Schulz, are two miles from here, and I happen to know they're away for the month. A rental cabin, owned by the Hamiltons, is another half mile from there, but it's closed up right now."

"I didn't fall out of the sky," she said with frustration. Although her body felt as if she had.

"Probably not, which means you had to come from the road off the main highway, and that's way too far from the creek for you to have walked in the storm. Since there's no car, that means someone brought you."

Her eyes popped open. "And left me?"

"Appears that way."

"But why would—" She stopped suddenly as a thought came to her. Eyes wide, she stared at Caleb, her fingers nervously working at the top button of her shirt. "Do you think...is it possible that someone wanted to—"

She couldn't finish. It suddenly hurt to breathe. She looked away, struggling to hold on to her composure, but with a will of its own, her body started to shake.

"No." He took hold of her shoulders and forced her to look at him. "There was no indication of someone hurting you like that."

"How would you know?" she whispered hoarsely.

"When I brought you in last night, you were covered with mud."

Confused, she looked at him. "And?"

"And I had to clean you up. Your clothes weren't torn that way."

"Oh...I see." She *was* beginning to see. Too clearly. Up to now, she'd been too confused, too disoriented to have given a great deal of thought to her current condition and clothing. "So last night...you had to, that is you—"

"Had to be done, Sarah. You were soaking wet, covered with an inch of mud, and bleeding. I had to get you out of your clothes and in the shower, not only to get you clean and see how badly you were hurt, but to warm you up. You'll have to trust me that I was a perfect gentleman."

Trust him? Yes, she did have to trust him. What choice did she have? Still, the thought of him, a stranger, taking off her clothes, seeing her naked like that—

Suddenly the image—no, more like the sensation—
of a man's wet, bare skin against her own came to her
again, just as it had last night when she'd awakened
the first time. Only this time she understood where it
came from. Her face blossomed bright red. Her
mouth dropped open as she stared at him. "Did you,
were you also—"

"'Fraid so. It was the quickest and easiest way. I was
almost as wet and muddy as you, and I've never taken
a shower with my clothes on yet."

She looked quickly away as humiliation burned
clear down to her toes. "Oh, my."

Cupping her chin with his fingertips, he lifted her
face to his and smiled. "If you have a husband, I'm a
dead man," he teased.

*A husband?* Did she have one? And if she did,
would she be so incredibly aware of Caleb right now?
The musky scent of his skin, the heat of his body, the
touch of his hand on her chin? She stared at his lips
and felt a strange tingling through her body. "I owe
you my life," she said quietly.

He moved closer, and she felt the warmth of his
breath on her cheek. "And Wolf."

She smiled at that.

His hand dropped away. "We'll give it a couple of
days. You'll either remember who you are, or someone will be looking for you."

"What if there's no one?" Her smiled faded.
"What if no one claims me?"

Her worry cut straight to his heart. He understood,
more than she could ever know. He saw himself
twenty-five years ago, nine years old. Alone. Sepa-
rated from Carrie, waiting for foster parents that never
showed up. "Everyone has someone."

Her gaze leveled with his. "Do you?"

His jaw clenched. "No."

Utter despair darkened her soft blue eyes, and he kicked himself for not lying.

"Why are you doing this?" she asked. "Helping someone you don't know?"

Good question. He could tell her it was because she might be a government agent who had amnesia and it wouldn't be a good idea to turn her in to the police. Or he could tell her it was because he'd help out anyone in trouble. But, of course, that was a lie.

He looked at her, watched her anxiously searching his face and decided there was really only one answer. Strangely enough, it was an honest one.

"I don't know."

She nodded, seemingly accepting that answer. "What about your work, or whatever it is you do here? Won't I be in the way?"

"I'm in insurance," he said carefully. "Life insurance. I broke my shoulder, and I'm on medical leave right now." Mostly true, he thought. His business was a form of insurance, and he had broken his shoulder.

She sighed heavily, then ran her hands through her hair as she stared at the fire.

"Hey, Hunter," she said after a long moment.

"Yeah?"

"Since you saved me, do you think you could feed me, too? I'm starving."

# Three

___

Sarah sat at the small kitchen table, her gaze focused on the plate of spaghetti in front of her. She pushed the pasta around her dish, listening to the sound of the rain on the roof. She'd been starving a half hour ago, before she'd washed up and made herself presentable, but her appetite had waned the minute she'd sat across from Caleb, and the full realization of her isolation with the man hit her.

Alone.

With a man she didn't know, had never even seen before. At least, she *thought* she'd never seen before. She'd tried to remember what had happened to her, how she'd come to be here in this condition, but every time she'd tried, the pain in her head had become unbearable.

She watched Caleb as he ate, amazed at his appetite and his ability to accept this situation so calmly. As if strange women fell at his doorstep all the time. Which, considering the man's looks, might very well be the case.

"Thank you for the clothes and the, uh, other things you bought for me in town today," she said, appreciative of the boots and jeans and denim shirt he'd picked up for her. She hadn't tried them on yet, but they appeared to be the right sizes. He'd also bought her some personal items which included, much to her continued embarrassment, underwear and toiletries. "Please be sure and keep the receipt so I can reimburse you."

He took a long swig of milk, then set the glass down with a clunk. "That might be difficult since I stole most of it."

"You what!"

He looked at her with the patience one reserves for a child. "I couldn't very well buy ladies' clothes and underwear without raising a few eyebrows. Pinewood is a small town. Everyone knows who I am, and that I live alone. Unless I want people here to wonder if I'd picked up some unusual habits, I thought it best to be discreet."

"Stealing is discreet?"

"Necessary. If it makes you feel better, I dropped a few bills behind the market counter. Judy will find it, and since she owns the store, it will go into her pocket."

An honest crook. That should make her feel better, but it only increased the burning sensation in her stomach. In spite of her discomfort, she was pleased with the clothes and other items. Having a few things of her own gave her a small sense of identity. Other than the sweater and skirt she'd had on when he found her, which Caleb had washed and hung up in the shower to dry, she had nothing. Even her shoes had been lost in the storm.

She rubbed her feet together, thankful for the socks he'd given her to wear. They were way too big, but soft and warm, like the thermal pants and cotton shirt she also had on. *His* thermal pants and cotton shirt. Her stomach fluttered at the thought.

"Is Judy a friend of yours?" she asked cautiously.

He shrugged, then scooped up some spaghetti sauce with a piece of bread and took a bite.

Suddenly worried, she poked at a green bean. "Close personal?"

One brow raised, he looked at her.

She straightened and lifted her chin, irritated he was making her inquiry so difficult. "This is a rather delicate situation, Caleb. I'm in your home, wearing your clothes. I believe I should at least be prepared for the possibility of a jealous lover bursting through the door."

"Ah." He chewed thoughtfully. "You think Judy will be upset we took a shower together?"

"We did not shower together!"

"We didn't?"

"Not like that, and you know it." He was teasing, making jokes. Her fingers tightened around the fork in her hand. "You may find my anxiety amusing, Mr. Hunter, but I find it extremely uncomfortable."

"Sarah, Judy is eighty-four years old and has no teeth." He made an effort to look serious, but it was a weak one. "Are you really that embarrassed I saw you naked?"

She nearly choked. How could he be so blasé about this? "Showering with a strange woman may be an everyday occurrence for you, but I assure you it most certainly is not for me!"

He smiled. "I find that extremely encouraging."

Flustered, she drew in a sharp breath and glared at him. "You know what I mean. I don't shower with strange men."

His smile slowly faded. "Well, you can't really be sure about that now, can you? Unless you remember something and you're holding out on me."

It was back. That look of mistrust. An imperceptible tightening of his voice and mouth. And his eyes. A cold flash of wariness and doubt. She had the inexplicable feeling that anyone who might cross this man would find themselves in serious danger.

"I don't remember anything, Caleb. I wish to God I did. I could be a beautician or a grape picker for all I know. But whatever I am, I'm not like that, I mean, I'm not a, uh, I'm not—"

"Loose?" he supplied.

She blushed furiously. "Yes."

Caleb sighed. "Just my luck. A beautiful, sexy woman falls into my arms, and I can't do anything about it."

Sarah straightened in her chair and stared at the food on her plate. "Don't tease me like that," she said quietly.

"Like what?"

"I'm not beautiful, and I'm certainly not sexy."

She had to be kidding, Caleb thought, watching Sarah push her green beans into a little mountain. Her blond hair fell in natural waves around her heart-shaped face, and wisps of the silken strands framed her wide, soft blue eyes. He knew women who would kill for the long thick lashes and smooth skin she had.

Why would she possibly think she wasn't attractive? Even in an oversize man's shirt and loose-fitting thermal pants she was one of the most alluring women he'd ever seen.

He took a bite of pasta and studied her carefully for a moment. She held her shoulders stiff, her eyes carefully averted from his. Her cheeks were bright red. Strange, he couldn't remember the last time he'd been around a woman who blushed.

"So what *do* you think?" he asked, leaning back in his chair. "What kind of a person do you think you were—are?"

She looked up at him, and he saw the distress in her eyes. "I don't know."

"A secretary, maybe? Having an affair with the boss, who tries to off you before his wife found out?"

Her eyes flashed blue fire. "Certainly not! I would never have an affair with a married man."

"A housewife, then?" he went on. "With six children, married to a double-dealing drug lord whose rivals want to make an example out of you."

Her lips pressed tightly together. "I don't have a husband or children."

"And how do you know?"

"I just know."

Did she? he wondered. Was she holding something back on him? Or was the whole thing a lie? She looked so damn innocent. If she was an agent and this was an act, she was very, very good.

And if she was lying, he resolved—about anything—he'd find out. That was one thing he *was* sure about.

"Okay." He pushed his plate away and let his gaze roam over her. "So what do we know about you, then?"

"I'm not sure what you mean."

He stared at her face, forcing himself to stay focused on the facts and not the curve of her soft lips.

"Well, for one thing, your age. I'd guess you're about twenty-four or five. Educated. Raised in the South, but left when you were a child. You're practical and efficient, and well-mannered."

She simply stared at him, eyes wide. "How could you possibly guess all that about me?"

He shrugged. "Your speech, the way you move, the clothes you were wearing."

"What about my clothes?" There was a touch of defensiveness in her voice.

"No name brands. Simple and conservative."

"Simple and conservative?"

What was it with women? he thought. He'd told her she was beautiful and she denied it; now he said her clothes were conservative and she was obviously offended. "Just an observation," he said flatly, "not a judgment."

"And what other *observations* have you, Mr. Holmes?"

She stabbed her fork into her spaghetti, and Caleb had the distinct feeling she would have preferred to stick the utensil in his chest. "Well, you're no grape picker or beautician, for one."

"Oh? And you know this because . . . ?" She lifted one brow, waiting for an explanation.

"Your hands."

"My hands?"

"Hands say a lot about a person. Yours don't see physical work, or a lot of water. Your skin is smooth, nails trimmed carefully, except for the ones that are broken right now. My guess is you were struggling to hold on to something. Maybe rocks or dirt or a tree. More than likely you fell, and that's when you hit your head."

"You sound more like a detective than an insurance agent," Sarah muttered. Still, his observations did intrigue her.

She laid her fork down and spread her hands out in front of her. He was right, she thought dimly. Other than the scratches on her palms and knuckles, her skin was soft and unlined, her fingers long and slender. She stared at her jagged, broken nails, trying to picture them as they would have been before last night....

The pounding in her head started up again. Her hands suddenly lost focus. The room around her dissolved.

*Dark. It was so dark, so cold. Rain pelted her face.*

She no longer stared at her hands, but another's. A man's. Grabbing her...trying to pull her backward...

She bit him, sank down hard with her teeth into the flesh under his thumb until she tasted blood. Furious, he howled and let go.

She fell.

*Kill her if you have to... kill her... kill her...*

Sarah felt as if a steel band were squeezing her chest. She couldn't breathe. Couldn't think. She closed her eyes, terrified she might remember, terrified she wouldn't. Emotions she didn't understand filled her. Betrayal, fear, shock.

She cried out as two large hands grabbed her shoulders.

"Sarah!"

Shaking, she opened her eyes and met Caleb's concerned gaze. "I bit him. His hand," she whispered. "He wants me dead."

"Who, Sarah?" Caleb knelt beside her. "Tell me who."

"He's so angry." The man's voice in her head was perfectly clear now. As furious as it was ruthless. "So...cold."

He tightened his hold on her arms. "Give me a name, a face."

She opened her mouth, waiting for the answer to drop down like a gum ball out of a machine. But there was nothing. Empty. No face, no name. Just a disembodied voice. All she could do was shake her head.

Something crashed against the back door of the kitchen. Sarah screamed and jumped into Caleb's arms.

"It's all right." He held her for a moment, then stood. "It's just Wolf."

Caleb opened the door and Wolf ran in, spraying water as he shook his fur.

Sarah's eyes widened at the sight of something in the animal's jaws, and when he leapt toward her, she shrank back. Tail wagging, Wolf laid the dark, soggy object at Sarah's feet. She couldn't bear to look. She knew cats often brought "gifts" to their owners, but the thought of a live offering from a wolf was just too much. She squeezed her eyes shut.

"Sarah," Caleb said gently. "Open your eyes."

She shook her head.

"It's all right, open them."

She peeked through slitted eyelids, then opened her eyes wide and stared down at a woman's black shoe.

Her shoe.

Two days later, after the storm finally passed, Caleb found the shoe's mate.

He stood at the bottom of a steep cliff and stared up at the craggy hillside. A fifty-foot wall of sharp, jagged rocks and boulders glared back. Six feet up, directly above where he'd found the shoe, a piece of navy blue fabric, captured on the branch of a boxwood, flapped in the afternoon breeze like a tiny flag. Sarah's skirt.

She'd fallen here.

It was unbelievable she hadn't been killed or more seriously injured. Surviving the fall had been amazing enough, but the fact she'd then managed to walk along the bank of the creek and end up so close to his cabin was a miracle.

His hand tightened around the shoe in his hand. Fear could do that. Drive a person to an act of near supernatural proportion. And based on the fear he'd seen in her eyes two days ago in the kitchen when she'd had a flashback, she'd been terrified.

He hadn't pressed her for information since that time. She'd needed to rest and had spent most of the past two days sleeping. Her headaches were gone now, and the wound on her head was healing well. When he'd left the cabin a little while ago, she'd just gone into the bathroom. At the sound of the shower door closing and the water spraying, Caleb had been all too reminded of her slender, curved body, and how long he'd been cooped up in the cabin. He'd had to get out of there, fast, and had decided the time was right to retrace her steps of the other night.

He stared up at the cliff again and watched the shimmering descent of several aspen leaves caught on the breeze. They landed at his feet, then scattered over a bed of damp pine needles.

The main road was at the top of the cliff.

Had she been thrown from a car up there and slid down here? Or had she accidentally fallen?

Or the other possibility, one he still had a hard time believing: was she an agent, and the entire situation a fabrication? It would certainly require dedication to go to the lengths she had gone to get to him, but there were agents of that caliber. He'd been one once. Men and women who would give their lives, their souls, for their job. Had she set this whole thing up, then been a victim of her own plan?

He certainly wouldn't have any answers standing around here all day, he thought with annoyance. The rain would have washed away any tire tracks or footprints at the top, but there might be something, some little piece of evidence up there.

He could either climb up or walk back to the cabin and drive to the main road.

He thought of Sarah, humming in the shower when he'd left, hot water spraying down on her, and decided physical exercise might be the best direction.

He tossed her shoe down, dug one boot into the soft dirt, then reached for the closest rock to pull himself up.

And froze.

Someone was watching him.

He knew the feeling too well to ignore it. It crept up his spine and over his neck. Casually, he bent down as if to tie his shoe, then reached slowly into the light jacket he wore and pulled out his gun.

A movement from a nearby tree had him dropping to the ground.

"Come out in the open," he said with deadly intensity. "Now!"

Sarah stepped out.

The swear word he uttered was quite raw and to the point.

"What the hell are you doing here?" He lowered his gun.

"I—" Her voice caught, and her eyes were still on the gun as she took another step out. "A walk," she finally managed to say. "I was taking a walk."

She wore the jeans and boots he'd brought her, and her own tan pullover sweater. It was impossible not to notice the snug fit of the jeans over her rounded hips and long legs, or the rise of her breasts under the sweater.

He'd spent two nights tossing and turning on the couch, just thinking about her in his bed, still wearing his shirt and thermal underwear. That first night, when he'd watched her mend her skirt by the fire, she'd handled the needle and thread with an expertise that made him wonder if she might be a seamstress. When he'd started to fantasize about those fingers moving over his own skin, he'd busied himself in the kitchen.

Tentatively she moved closer, and he noticed her hair was still damp from her shower. The breeze picked up the strands curling around her flushed face. With a sigh he slipped his gun back into his jacket.

"You shouldn't be out here," he said more sharply than he'd intended. He wondered himself if it was concern or annoyance. Both, perhaps.

"I couldn't stay inside anymore, Caleb," she said. "It's too beautiful out here."

"And what if someone is looking for you? Someone you *don't* want to find you. Don't you think this would be the first place they'd come to?"

Her gaze flicked to his, and he saw the fear there. "I—I hadn't thought of that."

"Think about it."

He was right, Sarah told herself. It was stupid to come out in the open, knowing that someone wanted to kill her. And she knew now, without a doubt, that someone *had* tried to kill her, just as she knew, somehow, that he would try again.

She'd just needed to get out of the cabin, if only for a few minutes. She'd walked along the creek bank, following Wolf most of the way, until he'd been sidetracked by a squirrel. When she'd spotted Caleb, she'd impulsively hidden behind the tree.

It was silly, she knew, watching him like that. But in the time she'd spent awake at the cabin with him, she'd never been able to really look at him. Not without him looking back at her with those dark, intense eyes. Eyes that made her shiver inside, a mixture of fear and something else, something not entirely unpleasurable. And other than the time that first day when he'd crawled into bed with her in an attempt—an extremely successful attempt, she might add—to shake her up, he hardly seemed to notice her. In fact she thought that he was making a point to stay away from her.

Instinctively she knew she'd never met a man like Caleb before. Every move he made, every word he spoke, was calculated, determined. He was not a man who trusted easily, men or women, and she sensed he still didn't trust her. At times she felt he was annoyed by her intrusion into his life, other times, amused. Most of the time he frightened her.

And at the same time he fascinated her.

She watched as he reached down and picked something up. A shoe—the missing shoe. *Her* missing shoe.

"Did you find that here?"

He nodded. "Feeling a little like Cinderella?" he asked dryly.

She looked at the wet, muddy shoe and her jeans. "After midnight, definitely."

He smiled, something he rarely did, Sarah thought. And a good thing it was, she decided, based on the flutter in her stomach his smile elicited. She took the shoe from him and examined it. "How were you able to find it?"

"It made sense you would have stayed close to the creek that night, which turns too narrow right here to follow any direction but toward the cabin. This cliff leads straight up to the main road into town."

She glanced up at the cliff and tightly clutched her shoe. "Did I . . . is this where . . ."

"Where you fell." He pointed to a shrub a few feet up. "There's a piece of your skirt stuck on that branch right there."

Her hand moved up to touch the gold necklace at her throat. "It's so steep . . . so high," she whispered.

He nodded grimly. "The rocks were wet and slippery. You must have slid down, catching yourself on boulders and rocks and mud to break your speed. Plus

I see a few broken shrubs. They must have slowed you down, as well.''

*Dear Lord, how did I survive a fall like this?* It felt as if her blood had turned to ice as she stared at the piece of fabric caught on the branch. It flapped in the breeze, waving wildly at her, and she pictured herself coming down the cliff, no control, nothing to hang on to, nowhere to go but down.

This wasn't like *Cinderella* at all, she thought, but *Alice in Wonderland,* and a quote from the story popped into her mind: "Down, down, down...too dark to see anything...after such a fall as this I shall think nothing of tumbling down stairs..."

The same images came back to her, the ones she'd had in the kitchen. The angry voice, the taste of blood in her mouth, the rain.

"Sarah."

She blinked and looked at Caleb. She hadn't even realized that he'd taken her arm and set her down on a smooth boulder, then knelt beside her.

"Are you remembering something?" he asked.

She shook her head slowly. "Nothing I haven't told you already."

He watched her for a long moment, as if he were weighing a decision very carefully. His hand, still wrapped around her arm, tightened a fraction, and the heat of his fingers seeped all the way through her thick sweater.

"Sarah," he said slowly, "I want to try something, but you have to agree to it, and in order to agree, you have to trust me."

Something in his eyes, the tone of his voice, sent a chill through her. She'd trusted him up to this point because she'd really had no choice. Now he was giving her a choice. He wanted her to trust him willingly. Completely.

Could she?

Her throat constricted as she stared back at him and saw the grim set of his mouth. If he'd wanted to hurt her, he could have several times over. He still could. Though she'd healed considerably, she was still weak, and even in the best of health, how could a small woman possibly defend herself against a six-foot-three man built from solid muscle?

She couldn't.

She was nearly as helpless now as she had been when he'd found her. He hadn't hurt her then, and he wouldn't hurt her now.

She drew in a slow breath, met his somber gaze and nodded.

He stood, then pulled her up beside him. "Close your eyes and no matter what, don't open them."

She did as he asked. The scent of the mountains closed in around her; pine and damp earth. And Caleb. He moved closer to her and she smelled him— a mixture of warm, masculine skin and the faint odor of a spicy after-shave.

She heard the rustle of leaves and the snap of a twig as he moved behind her. "I'm going to put my arm around you."

Her heart started to pound. He was recreating that night, trying to break through her amnesia and force her to remember. His arm came around her, circling her shoulders, drawing her close against her broad, muscled chest.

"It's raining." His breath fanned over her ear. "You're cold and frightened."

She *was* frightened, though certainly not because she remembered anything about that night. It was Caleb she was frightened of, or more truthfully, herself, and the reaction she was having to the contact of their bodies: a swirling sensation low in her belly. Her skin felt tight, her breathing shallow. She felt his body tighten, as well, and the lightest brush of his mouth against her ear. She shivered.

"There's thunder," he said hoarsely, "and lightning. The ground is muddy under your shoes, and it's hard to walk."

She tried to focus, to concentrate, but with Caleb pressed so close, and the hot rush of his breath down her neck, it was impossible. Her knees felt weak, and it was all she could do not to turn in his arms and face him, to rise up and press her lips to his.

Without warning he tightened his hold and yanked her against him. She gasped at the sudden movement.

"It's dark," he said roughly, "you want to get away from me. You know I'm going to kill you."

She struggled against him, kicking out with her feet. But he was too strong. She might as well be a fly with its wings snipped.

*Kill her . . . kill her . . . dammit, don't let her get away . . .*

The darkness rose up to meet her. Rain pounded her face. She twisted frantically and screamed, saw herself being dragged back toward a car, knowing she was dead if they reached it. She bit him, hard, and when he released her, she swung around.

And kicked him as hard as she could between the legs.

# Four

Caleb wondered why he was seeing stars when it was the middle of the day. He also wondered why he was sitting on his butt on the cold, damp earth, trying to suck air into lungs that suddenly didn't work.

"Caleb!"

He heard his name, but the explosion of pain in his body made it impossible to answer.

"Oh, my God, Caleb!" He felt cool hands touch his face. "Are you all right?"

*All right?* Was he *all right?* Of *course* he wasn't all right.

"I'm so sorry," he heard Sarah say. "I didn't think, I mean, I just didn't realize—"

He drew in a long gulp of air, then blinked several times. Her face came into focus, a few inches away from his own. Her eyes were dark with worry, her brow furrowed.

He'd never expected her to move that fast, or with such *intensity.* He realized with immense relief that her hit had not been a direct one or he'd be flat on his back.

"Caleb, please," she said frantically, "speak to me, say something."

"I'm fine," he said in a tiny high voice. "Perfectly all right."

"Oh, no, Caleb, I'm sorry." She knelt beside him and cupped his face in her hands. Her fingers were soft and smooth against his cheeks. He could breathe again now, and the pain began to subside.

"Did I really hurt you?" she asked.

He hardly wanted to admit she'd hurt his...ego. He doubted she weighed more than one-fifteen; he was closer to two-twenty. Not to mention he had a black belt and had been trained to expect the unexpected.

The truth was that when he'd held her against him, felt her slender body tucked intimately to his, he hadn't thought of anything except the curve of her rear end against the lower portion of his body and how sweet her hair and skin smelled after her shower. Desire had shot through him like a rocket out of control. A rocket that had suddenly crashed, he reminded himself.

"I'm all right," he said with more annoyance than he intended.

"Are you sure?" She glanced down, then quickly looked back into his face as she realized where her gaze had gone.

"Well," he said with a drawl, "if it'll make you feel better, we could take a test drive to check things out."

It took a beat for his meaning to sink in, then her cheeks grew red. "You're definitely all right," she said with a frown.

Her hands slid away from his face, and she started to stand, but he reached for her and pulled her back. "You remembered something."

Her skin, flushed with embarrassment only a moment ago, now turned pale. She sank back down beside him, onto a blanket of pine needles and leaves, then drew in a long, slow breath and stared blankly at the hands she'd spread over her knees.

"It's like looking into a shattered mirror," she said after a moment. "Incomplete images and faces. Nothing has definition, just jagged pieces."

"Tell me, Sarah," he said. "Tell me what you see."

Her brow furrowed, as if in pain, and she lifted her gaze to his. "He let go of me when I bit him, then I—" she swallowed hard and moisture formed in her eyes "—I turned and kicked my knee up as hard as I could."

Caleb watched a tremor shiver through Sarah. He covered her hand with his; her fingers were like ice. "I hope you scored a bull's-eye with the bastard," he said tightly.

Her lips curved upward. "Me, too."

Giving—or receiving—comfort had always been foreign to Caleb, but when he saw her begin to shake, he pulled her into his arms with a movement as natural as breathing. She buried her face into his shoulder, and he felt the wetness of her tears through his shirt.

"I'm frightened," she whispered hoarsely.

"No one's going to hurt you." He tucked her head under his chin and smoothed her hair away from her face. "I didn't pull you out of the mud for nothing, you know."

He felt her soft laugh against his chest, then a small sob. His chest tightened at the sound of her distress. What was it about this woman that made him want to leap tall buildings and catch bullets with his teeth? He tried to tell himself he'd do the same, feel the same, for any woman in the same situation, but he knew that wasn't the truth. His job had required he safeguard at least a dozen women in equally threatening situations, and he'd never felt anything like this before. This didn't feel like a job.

This felt personal.

And even now, as he drew her closer to him, he tried to tell himself she wasn't his problem, that he should take her to the sheriff and let him take care of her. But his gut told him that would be a mistake, that he might just be signing her death warrant.

She pulled away from him suddenly, her tear-filled eyes wide. "You said it was dangerous for me out here, that someone might be looking for me. That means I might be putting you in danger, too. I can't stay here anymore."

She started to rise, but he caught her arms and gently tugged her back. "Sarah, you don't have to worry about me, I'm—"

*I'm what? A special agent for the United States Government trained to deal with all types of terrorists and criminals?* She not only wouldn't believe him, she'd think he'd gone crazy himself. No, this was hardly the time to tell her. And for that matter, she didn't ever need to know.

"I'm more than capable of taking care of myself," he said.

She shook her head and laid her hands on his chest. "But you don't know, you can't be sure. I can't let you take a chance like that."

Her words stunned him, and at the same time, touched a part of him that he'd thought long dead. When was the last time someone had cared about him, really cared about him?

She stared at him, her bright eyes earnest, her lips set in a straight, determined line. He suddenly couldn't take his gaze off those lips. Her scent filled his senses; a clean, light fragrance that was hers alone, as potent as it was seductive.

He looked back into her eyes, eyes as pale blue as an early morning sky. He watched them darken as she held his gaze. Her lips parted in wonder. Neither one of them moved.

The breeze swirled leaves around their legs; the rushing water from the creek echoed through the pine trees; a squirrel chattered from a nearby branch.

And still neither one of them moved.

"What's happening, Caleb?" she whispered.

Nothing he understood. Or maybe he didn't want to understand. Whatever it was, it was as strong as it was sharp, a need that overpowered reason or logic. His hands tightened on her arms and she swayed toward him.

"You don't even know who I am," she said raggedly. "*I* don't know who I am."

"That doesn't seem to matter," he said, and lowered his mouth to hers.

She tasted like cool mint and warm sunlight. Her hands spread over his chest, and her sigh was as soft as the breeze curling around them. *Insane.* That's what this was. He had no right to kiss this woman, to hold her in his arms like this and take advantage of her vulnerability.

He pulled her closer and deepened the kiss.

His mouth played over hers, hungry to taste more of her. She responded, tentatively touching her tongue to his. There it was again, he thought. That innocence. Enticing as it was intriguing. A sweetness that would send any man, sane or not, over the edge.

And when she slid her arms around his neck and pressed closer to him, that's exactly where he was. Over the edge.

Time or place ceased to exist for Sarah. She heard the distant sound of birds, then her own voice, soft and faraway, whispering a name. *Caleb.* She was a stranger not only to him, but to herself, her own body. The feelings careening through her were foreign to her, yet familiar somehow, at a primitive, subconscious level. They frightened and excited at the same time. Her breasts, pressed against Caleb's muscled chest, felt full and tight, and she realized she wanted him to touch her, not only there, but everywhere. The mere thought of his hands on her skin sent shivers of anticipation through her that centered low in her belly and sharpened. Had a man ever touched her like this before? Could she have ever forgotten a pleasure as incredible as this?

She'd lost her mind as well as her memory, she thought desperately. Why else would she so wantonly respond to Caleb as she was? Nothing could ever come of this. Nothing. She would remember who she was, why she was here, and she'd be gone. Back to wherever it was she came from. Back to her life.

But she was responding, completely, without restraint, as if being here with Caleb was the most natural, real thing in the world. The *only* real thing amidst the overwhelming turmoil and confusion.

His mouth moved anxiously over her lips, insistently, relentlessly. She opened to him, trembling with anticipation, then suddenly she was on her back, the cool, damp ground underneath her and the scent of damp leaves and pine filling her senses. He kissed her deeply, arching his body over hers, and she surged upward to meet him, wrapping her arms tightly around his neck. Need twisted and knotted inside her, and when his hand slid up under her sweater and he cupped one breast in his palm, the knots tightened with exquisite pain.

She moaned, squirming beneath him restlessly, wanting more, desperate to have him closer, to remove the barrier of clothing and feel him against her, inside her. She moaned again, though in her haze of pleasure she thought the sound was more of a whimper, a plea for him to hurry. And when his mouth closed over her breast, caressing the soft flesh through her thin cotton bra, there were no thoughts at all, just mindless, pure sensations.

Wolf barked sharply from somewhere close by, and Caleb froze. Swearing under his breath, he moved away from her, then slowly rose. Sarah stared at him, her body and mind screaming for him to come back to her. With a heavy sigh he pulled her to her feet.

"I shouldn't have done that," he said hoarsely, staring down at her with intense dark eyes.

*Shouldn't have done that?* Had he really said that? Sarah looked quickly away, refusing to give in to the tears of embarrassment burning her eyes. If she'd ever wished the earth would simply open and swallow her up, she couldn't have wished it more than she did at this moment. How could she have let herself get so carried away like that, rolling on the ground with a man she hardly knew? And if he hadn't stopped when he had, then Lord only knew what they'd be doing!

But she did know. Exactly what she'd wanted him to do. What she still wanted him to do.

"I'd better get back," she said, brushing at the leaves on her clothes, hoping he wouldn't see how her hands were shaking. "I'm feeling a little tired, and I wanted to fix dinner and—"

"Sarah." He took hold of her arm. "I'm sorry. That shouldn't have happened."

*Shouldn't have done that* was bad enough. Now it was *I'm sorry,* and *it shouldn't have happened.* She drew in a slow breath and pulled her arm away. "I'm sorry, too, Caleb. I've caused you nothing but trouble since you took me in. I'll find a way to repay you, I promise."

Certain she was going to make an even bigger fool out of herself, Sarah hurried away before he could answer.

It was almost dark by the time Caleb returned to the cabin. The smell of wood smoke filled the air and something else, something distinctly familiar and incredibly wonderful. *Bread baking,* he realized. Wolf followed him into the cabin, sniffed at the air, then made a beeline for the kitchen. No loyalty with that animal when it came to food, Caleb thought with a shake of his head. Not that he blamed him. If he hadn't made such a fool out of himself this afternoon, he'd be fast on the animal's heels.

But he *had* made a fool out of himself. Sarah was alone, vulnerable. Confused. She'd turned to him for help, not to be seduced. She had a life somewhere, a family. He had no right taking advantage of her or her innocence.

And she *was* innocent. He'd sensed her inexperience that first day when she'd wakened and he'd touched her, but today he'd felt it—a spark of hidden passion that had suddenly burst into flame. And it was that very innocence that had fueled his own desire. A desire that hadn't diminished, but had only grown since he'd tasted her.

He'd made a mistake. One he had no intention of making again. Once he got her fingerprint report back from Mike, he'd send her back home, wherever, and to whomever, that was.

"Caleb?"

She called him from the kitchen, and it startled him how just the sound of her voice made his pulse pick up. He'd never had a home, a real home, where a woman greeted him at the end of a day. He felt an unfamiliar warmth in his chest and realized he was actually smiling.

His smile faded. Sarah, like this home, was temporary, he reminded himself. Anything else was a fantasy. A warm fire and the smell of baking bread were luxuries he couldn't afford to grow accustomed to.

He started to turn, thinking he'd go back outside and let the cold air clear his mind. But then she stood in the kitchen doorway, and he could barely move. She'd taken off her sweater and was wearing the denim shirt again, with the sleeves rolled to her elbows. She'd also taken off her boots and slipped on a pair of white socks. He stared at those socks, *his* socks, that stretched over her small feet and disappeared into her jeans. It was hardly a picture that fantasies were made of, and yet the sight of her standing there, her gaze shy, her cheeks flushed, hit him like a sledgehammer straight to the gut.

"Dinner's almost ready," she said hesitantly. "I'll put it on the table while you wash up."

He nodded, and when she disappeared back into the kitchen, he washed, then ran a comb through his hair. She was setting a bowl of carrots next to a plate of pork chops when he came back into the kitchen. Wolf was by the back door, busy gulping down a bowl of dog food Sarah had given him.

"You didn't have to do this," he said, moving beside her.

She glanced at him, then quickly looked away. "I need to do something. You not only saved my life, you've taken care of me and fed me. I'm feeling better now, and cooking a meal is the least I can do."

He noticed a spot of flour on her neck, imagined how soft and smooth her skin would feel if he licked off the white powder. He had a brief, lustful thought about several things she could do for him, none of which included food.

"I've got the potatoes warming in the oven," she said hurriedly. "I hope you like mashed, but they're a little lumpy because I didn't know if you had an electric mixer, and I didn't want you to think I'd snoop through your cupboards, but the pork chops were in the freezer, and I saw the yeast and flour next to the dishes, so I thought I'd surprise you and . . ."

She continued to ramble about the food preparation while she grabbed two pot holders and pulled the potatoes out of the oven, apologizing that the food probably wasn't going to taste very good and her feelings wouldn't be hurt if he didn't eat it. She'd carefully avoided looking at him while she was rattling on, and he realized she was nervous.

He also knew why.

Despite his better judgment, he reached for her hand as she set the bowl of steaming potatoes on the table. She stiffened at his touch.

"Sarah," he said gently, "I think we better talk about what happened this afternoon or neither one of us is going to enjoy this meal."

He watched her fingers tighten around the green terry cloth pot holders in her hands. She stared at the hot pads and nodded slowly.

"I'm sorry," she said softly. "I don't know what came over me."

*She* was apologizing to him? Confused, he simply stared at her.

"I'm sure I wasn't like that before," she went on. "Maybe the hit on my head has caused me to be a wanton woman."

*A wanton woman?* It was obvious she was serious, and he tried very hard not to laugh. He'd seen more than his share of "wanton women" and she most definitely was not one of them. If he tried to tell her, would she even understand that no woman, wanton or not, had ever made him lose control like that? That he'd nearly taken her, right there in the forest, despite the fact that she might belong to someone else, despite the fact that he had no right?

"Sarah, look, you've got this all wrong—"

"I know I do." She twisted the pot holders. "I—I thought you wanted to kiss me. I thought that you, well, that you were—" She stopped then, her face a bright red.

"That I was what?"

"You know." She looked away. "Turned on."

The words were a whisper on her lips. And as he stared at those lips, he wanted nothing more than to drag her against him and show her just how right she was.

"I threw myself at you." She closed her eyes and drew in a long, slow breath. "I can't even imagine what you must think of me."

Obviously she couldn't imagine, Caleb thought in amazement. And if he pulled her against him right now, there would be little left to the imagination. But he'd learned his lesson once today already, and he knew if he did pull her into his arms and kiss her like he wanted, this time he wouldn't stop, consequences be damned.

"I'm not used to explaining or defending my actions," he said firmly. "Most of the time I don't much give a damn what anyone thinks, and I sure as hell don't give a damn what anyone says. But I want you to listen to me, and listen hard." He slipped one finger under her chin and forced her to look at him. "You're a beautiful woman—"

She shook her head. "You don't have to say that. I know I'm not—"

"Stop interrupting. You are a beautiful woman, and you didn't throw yourself at me this afternoon. I wanted to kiss you."

She stared at him, her baby blue eyes wide and soft. "You did?"

*Lord, don't look at me like that,* Caleb thought. "I wanted to do a hell of a lot more, too," he said, unable to stop himself as he ran his thumb over her jaw. "But I can't."

"You can't?"

"No." Damn, but she smelled good. A scent that was hers alone, a scent that triggered a response in him that left him aching. Her skin felt like silk under his fingers, and he nearly groaned as he realized that she'd leaned closer.

*The perfect seduction,* he thought, and with that thought came the doubt. She was too perfect. As if a computer had linked itself into his mind, tapped into his fantasies and created a woman he'd only dreamed about. A woman who was strong yet soft. Innocent yet passionate.

A woman he could trust.

But he couldn't trust her. He couldn't trust anyone. And even if he could, what difference would it make? She wasn't staying. She *couldn't* stay.

He sighed heavily and let his hand drop from her. "Sarah, you'll be leaving soon. If I'd made love to you earlier, or if I took you to my bed right now, I'd only be taking advantage of you. It would be a physical release, nothing else. And whatever you may think of yourself at the moment, I have the distinct feeling that sleeping with a man for sex alone is not something you would normally do."

Did she? Sarah wondered. She must, because she almost opened her mouth to argue the point with him. *I've done it again,* she thought miserably. *Made an idiot out of myself.* She was throwing herself at Caleb like some kind of floozy. She was almost afraid to get her memory back and find out exactly what kind of woman she was.

"No, of course not," she murmured. "I'm just a little...confused by everything that's happened, that's all." She stepped away awkwardly and pulled out a chair. "Why don't we eat...before it gets cold?"

He slid into the chair across from her and helped himself to a pork chop and potatoes, obviously unaffected by the exchange between them. He ate with enthusiasm, and when he bit into the fresh bread she'd baked, he even groaned with delight.

She stared at the mashed potatoes she'd put on her plate, but they may as well have been wet cement.

At least he was interested in her cooking, she thought with a silent sigh. And if he liked this, then she could make him a grilled garlic butter chicken that would make his mouth water and a crème brulée that would knock his socks off.

She smiled at the image, then went suddenly still. Her vision blurred, and a heavy, dull pain shot through her head.

How did she know how to cook like that?

*A kitchen. Wooden cows and sunflowers. Blue curtains . . .*

"Sarah?"

She heard Caleb call her, but she couldn't move.

"What is it?" he said gently. "Tell me what you see."

"My . . . house," she whispered. "My kitchen. My living room. Suitcases. I'm going somewhere . . . on a trip."

"Where?"

She closed her eyes. The pain increased in her temples.

"Where, Sarah?" Caleb asked again.

"The mountains?" She shook her head. "No, the ocean."

*She'd packed a bathing suit. Bright pink. Plants watered. Mail stopped. A knock at the door . . . her taxi? She moved toward the door, stopped at the sound of a low, deep growl...*

"Sarah!"

She opened her eyes, heard the knock again. Not in her mind this time, but coming from Caleb's front door. Wolf growled again. Caleb pointed a finger at Wolf and the animal immediately quieted.

The lines of Caleb's face were rigid when he turned back to her. "I want you to stay in the kitchen and keep out of sight. Don't say a word."

Eyes wide, she stared at him, then nodded slowly.

He pulled the door closed behind him as he left the kitchen. Knees shaking, Sarah moved to the door, quietly opening it an inch so she could see into the living room. She watched Caleb reach for the gun he kept on the mantel, then tug his shirt from his pants and slip the gun into his waistband before he opened the front door. She strained to see around him, but his large frame blocked her view.

"Sorry to bother you," Sarah heard an eerily familiar voice say. "But I was wondering if you've seen this woman."

Breath held, she watched Caleb take a picture from the man and look at it.

"Who is she?" Caleb asked.

"Sarah Phillips," the man replied. "My wife."

# Five

Caleb stared at the snapshot in his hand, a head shot of a woman. Her hair was pulled back, and she looked a couple of years younger, but it was definitely Sarah. Caleb looked back at the man standing in front of him. A little old for Sarah, Caleb thought irritably. He had short cropped blond hair, and stood at six-one or two. The man smiled, but it never reached his steel-gray eyes. There were two other men standing a few feet away, outside a black Suburban. They all wore hunting clothes and heavy jackets.

"Name's Sam." He held out his hand. "Sam Phillips. I'm staying a few miles away in the Kramer cabin."

The Kramer place was a part-time rental cabin on the other side of Pinewood, nearly five miles away, Caleb thought, accepting the man's hand. His palm was smooth, his fingers cold. He had the build of an athlete, but the hands of a pencil pusher.

Caleb instantly disliked him.

"You lost your wife?"

"It's a little complicated." He rubbed at his nose and shifted uncomfortably. "You see, she—Sarah—hasn't been well, so when my brother and cousin and I decided to come up to the mountains for a few days—" he pointed to the other men, who smiled stiffly "—well, I thought maybe the mountain air would help clear her mind a little. She's been very...confused lately."

Caleb handed the picture back. "Oh?"

Sam slipped the picture into his jacket pocket and sighed heavily. "She'd been in a...clinic since she miscarried the baby three months ago, but she hadn't had an episode for over a month, so I thought it would be safe to bring her home."

A knot grew in Caleb's stomach. Though he felt anything but, he folded his arms and leaned casually against the doorjamb, carefully blocking any view into the cabin. "Episode?"

"Paranoia," Sam said, shaking his head. "She imagines she's someone else, or people are after her. She's all right if she takes her medication, but I'm afraid she hasn't had it for a few days now."

It would explain so much, Caleb thought, forcing himself to appear friendly and relaxed. The men after her, her loss of memory.

"How long has she been missing?" he asked, glancing at the other men again. The shorter, stockier of the two wore a bandage on his right hand. Caleb made a mental note of the license plate on the car.

"Four days now," Sam said. "She'd told me she heard a storm was coming and she didn't want to stay in the mountains. She said she'd called a friend of hers to come pick her up and they were going to spend a few days in Santa Barbara. The phones weren't working during the storm, and by the time I reached the friend and found out that Sarah had never even called her, three days had already gone by. I've been searching for her since this morning."

Dammit! It made sense. Too much sense. "You think she's still around here?"

"I don't know. She's gone off on her own before, but she usually isn't away this long. I haven't called the authorities yet because I was so sure she'd show up by now, but I'm starting to worry that something may have happened to her."

*Starting* to worry? Anger surged through Caleb. This man's wife was missing for four days, and he was just *starting* to worry? He thought of Sarah, how frightened she'd been, how bruised and scratched she'd been when he'd brought her back to the cabin that night. His anger intensified, as did his protective feeling toward her.

All feelings he had no right to. Not if she was married to this man. And that was still the question . . . *if.* "You got a number I can call you at if I see her?" Caleb asked.

Sam reached into his shirt pocket and pulled out a card. "We're still at the cabin, but my calls are being forwarded from my office."

Caleb looked at the card. "Phillips Import. Los Angeles, California." There was an address and a phone number.

His jaw tightened. Everything this man told him made sense. The trauma of losing a baby could certainly have messed her up mentally. And if she had been confused, as Sam said, it was possible she'd wandered down the main road that far and accidentally fallen over the cliff. The shock to her body, combined with her emotional state, might have triggered her paranoia.

Dammit, anyway! The pieces fit together, too well, but the picture was wrong somehow. Or was he seeing a different picture because he didn't like the one right in front of his face?

He shouldn't—couldn't—let the fact that he was attracted to her and felt a certain responsibility for her, color his better judgment, which was to let her husband take care of her. Logic told him to turn Sarah over now.

His gut told him no.

"Hope you find her," Caleb said good-naturedly and shook Sam's hand again.

"Thanks." Sam smiled and turned to leave.

The sound of shattering glass from inside the cabin, then a small cry, stopped Sam. Eyes narrowed, he turned back around and stared at Caleb. The other men straightened.

Without missing a beat, Caleb called over his shoulder. "You okay, honey?" He heard a mumbled reply, then turned back to Sam. "My wife."

"Maybe I could talk to her." Sam stared hard at Caleb. "Just in case she's seen something."

Caleb's smile was cocky. "Only thing she's seen for the past two weeks is me. We just got married. And besides—" Caleb gave a conspiratorial wink "—this isn't exactly a good time, if you know what I mean."

Sam laughed, and the other two grinned. "Sorry to have bothered you," he said. "And congratulations."

"Thanks. I'll be sure and call you if we see anything."

Caleb closed the door, then watched at the window until the Suburban drove away. When he turned he saw Sarah standing in the kitchen doorway, her face ashen, arms held limply at her sides.

"I knocked over a glass on the counter," she said, her voice barely audible.

"You heard?"

"Yes."

"Tall guy, blond. Gray eyes." He handed her the card. "He had a picture of you, too."

Her hand shook as she stared at the business card. She lifted her gaze to his and asked quietly, "Why didn't you tell him about me?"

"I didn't like his haircut," Caleb said dryly.

She reached out and touched his arm, her eyes narrowed and pleading. "He's not my husband, Caleb. I may not know who I am, but I know I can't be married to that man, and I don't believe I was pregnant."

If she's been traumatized, Caleb thought grimly, denial would be her best defense—denial that she was ever pregnant or even that she'd been married.

He stared at her long, soft fingers clutching his arm. His skin burned where she touched him. "He knows you," Caleb said.

"Yes." She nodded slowly and let her hand drop away. "We've met somehow, I'm sure of that. I've heard his voice before. It scares me. Would I be afraid of my own husband?"

Her voice was small, almost childlike. He could have told her that a lot of women were afraid of their husbands, but she had enough to deal with at the moment. If Phillips was her husband, and he had hurt her, Caleb would make sure the man never hurt her again.

When she hugged her arms tightly to her, he started to reach for her, then stopped. He didn't dare touch her. There was too much emotion between them at the moment. He didn't know what he'd do if he touched her, and that frightened the hell out of him.

"I'm going into town," he said roughly. "I'll check it out. Don't go outside, don't answer the door."

He reached for his jacket and headed for the door, then stopped and turned back to her. "Sarah."

She looked at him, and the fear in her eyes almost made him go back to her. "What?"

"There's a gun in that drawer." He pointed to the end table by the couch. "If you need to, use it."

Sarah sat in front of the fire and stared blankly into the slowly dying flames. Wolf slept close by, his large black head nestled between his long, muscular legs. Caleb had been gone for over three hours, and every minute had seemed like a lifetime. A cuckoo clock over the mantel announced it was ten o'clock, and she listened to the persistent chirp as if it were speaking directly to her....

*Cuckoo...cuckoo...cuckoo...*

*Was* she crazy? She'd assured Caleb that she wasn't a lunatic on the run from a mental institution, but now she wasn't so sure.

Confusion closed over her like a heavy fog. All evening that man's words kept chipping away in her brain. *My wife... lost the baby... paranoia...*

Could it be? She drew in a long, shuddering breath and hugged her knees tightly to her. No! She refused to accept that that man—Sam Phillips—was her husband. And how could she possibly forget she'd lost a child? He was lying. She knew he was lying. But why? Why would someone make up such an elaborate story? There had to be a reason. *I've got to remember!*

And the voice, his *voice.* She squeezed her eyes shut and pressed her hands over her ears, wishing she could stop hearing the words. *Paranoia... paranoia... my wife... kill her... kill her...*

Her eyes flew open. Had he said those words? Was it possible that this was the man that had caused her accident? Heart pounding, she stared into the glowing red coals in the fireplace, willing herself to relax... to remember....

Rain. Lightning. Those things were clear in her mind. And the darkness. The headlights cut into the darkness no more than a few feet. *Headlights!* She was in a car... three men. An explosion... no, a flat tire. And then she was running. She slipped in the mud, and one of the men grabbed her. She bit him, then kicked.

*Kill her... kill her... kill her....*

And then she was falling—

"Sarah?"

She screamed and fell backward, raising her arm to ward off a blow, before she realized it was Caleb kneeling beside her. Her heart slammed against her chest. He took hold of her shoulders and steadied her.

"I . . . didn't hear you come in."

"You all right?" Concern furrowed his brow.

She drew in a slow, fortifying breath and nodded.

He sat beside her. Firelight shadowed his face, causing eerie shapes and contortions. There was no warmth in his eyes, only a cold, dark intensity. His mouth was set in a firm, hard line, and his touch was not the touch of a man who had kissed her earlier and desired her. It was the touch of an angry stranger.

"Tell me," she whispered. The words felt raw in her throat.

His gaze met hers. She felt a chill seep down clear to her bones.

"It checked out, Sarah," he said quietly. "Sam Phillips is your husband."

Caleb had no smelling salts; he certainly had never expected he would need them here in the mountains. A cool compress would have to do, he resolved, and pressed the wet washcloth to Sarah's forehead. He'd caught her when she'd fainted a minute ago, then laid her on the sofa. She'd felt so small in his arms, so fragile. And the look in her eyes before she'd passed out—like a frightened doe cornered by a grizzly bear.

And he was the grizzly bear.

He went into the kitchen and filled a glass with brandy, then moved back into the living room and stood over her. She lay so still, her breathing shallow, her skin pale as moonlight. With a mind of its own, his hand reached out and tucked a silky curl of hair behind her ear, then lightly traced the smooth line of her jaw. His chest constricted at the contact, and he quickly drew his hand away.

How could he hand his woman over to another man?

*Good God!* He staggered backward at the thought. *His woman?* He had no right to think of her as his. She wasn't a wounded kitten found in an alley, she was a woman. A *married* woman. He'd known from the beginning she had another life, that there was a possibility she had a husband. He thought of Phillips, and his stomach churned. He still couldn't believe that man was her husband, but Mike had checked everything out and it cleared.

Dammit, dammit, *dammit!*

Sarah stirred, then moaned softly. He sat beside her on the couch, and when her eyes fluttered open, he removed the washcloth from her forehead.

She rose on her elbows and stared at the glass in his hands. "I hope that's something strong."

He held the glass to her lips and she swallowed, then started to cough as the bitter liquid scorched her throat. He tossed back a long swallow himself.

"It's not true," she said hoarsely. "It can't be."

"A friend of mine pulled up your DMV and police file. Your maiden name is Grayson, married name Phillips. You live at 5234 Bedford Avenue in Valencia. There are no warrants or arrests, but as of a few hours ago the police are on alert to call your—" he hesitated, found he could barely say the word "—husband if you're picked up."

She hugged her arms to her and closed her eyes. "What else?"

A muscle jumped in his temple. "You're listed as mentally unstable."

She opened her eyes, and the hurt and fear he saw there cut through him like a knife. He struggled with every fiber of his being not to drag her into his arms.

"Paranoid." The word hung in the air.

He just stared at her and nodded.

"There's nothing I can say to convince you, is there?" Her shoulders slumped with defeat.

"You're in the computers, Sarah," he said. "You and Sam both. Even his importing business in Los Angeles was real."

"Computers lie, Caleb. Just like people." Her eyes went empty, blank. "You're going to take me back, aren't you?"

His hand tightened on the glass. He nodded.

"When?"

"In the morning."

"All right."

She swung her feet off the couch and stood. Her hand shook as she combed her hair away from her face. She moved silently toward the bedroom, then stopped at the doorway.

"I would have died without you, Caleb," she said quietly without turning around. "I want you to know I appreciate everything you've done for me."

She stepped into the bedroom and closed the door behind her. He stared at the glass in his hand and drained the contents.

Twenty minutes later Caleb was still staring at the same glass. He'd lost count how many times he'd refilled it, but it wasn't enough. Not yet. Not as long as his chest felt so damn tight and the look of betrayal in Sarah's eyes was still clear in his mind.

He *had* to take her back, dammit. What choice did he have? He'd followed Phillips and his buddies when he'd gone into town earlier, watched them as they'd had dinner at the Cougar Café. Phillips had played the part of worried husband well. He'd shown Sarah's picture to everyone, stuck to the same story he'd given Caleb, and he *had* filed a missing person's report. Caleb had discreetly checked with the sheriff and verified it.

And then he'd called Mike again and asked him to run a check on Sarah and Sam Phillips in California, using the plates from the Suburban. It was a match, right down to the fingerprints Caleb had sent Mike. According to the computer, Sarah was married to Sam Phillips. Caleb had even had Phillips's police records pulled to see if there were any reports of spouse abuse. Nothing.

Sarah needed help, he told himself. Once she remembered who she was, she'd be fine, happy even to return to her husband.

So why was his inner voice telling him—no, *screaming* at him—that something was wrong?

But was it his inner voice, or was it something else? He was attracted to Sarah; he wanted her. And he sure as hell didn't want her to belong to another man, even though he knew she could never belong to him. Was it his own inner desires that he'd denied for so long that had suddenly mutinied and refused to listen to reason?

But something *was* wrong. He knew it, he'd felt it the second he'd opened the door and found Phillips and his buddies there. He'd been too wound up to listen, and the possibility too unbelievable to accept.

*They were agents.*

The thought struck him like a lightning bolt. Good God, was it possible? They had the look, in their eyes, the way they stood, their mannerisms. Especially Phillips and the guy with the bandage on his hand.

Sarah had told him that she'd bitten one man's hand until she'd tasted blood. That would probably require stitches.

He ran a hand over his face and shook his head. It was too improbable, too implausible. He'd been working for the government too long, he thought, when he found conspiracy in a family drama. Everything had checked out. DMV, police, the business. He had no right interfering.

*Computers lie. Just like people.*

His eyes narrowed as he remembered Sarah's words.

*Computers lie . . . just like people . . .*

He sat up straighter. If people lied, of course computers could lie, too.

An agent had access to the average citizen's files. Computer records were easy to change, Caleb had done it himself when necessary.

He slammed the glass down on the coffee table and started for the bedroom door. He had to try. They'd stay up all night if they had to. Go over every detail again and again, until she did remember.

He didn't knock on the door, just opened it and stepped inside. The air inside the bedroom was cold. Too cold.

"Sarah."

She didn't respond. He moved beside the bed and flipped on the light.

She was gone.

Sarah stood at the edge of the dirt road, watching the moon as it slipped behind a bank of dark clouds.

Darkness closed over the forest. The wind whipped through her, then howled through the tops of the trees.

Shivering, she waited for the moon to appear again. The clouds had been gathering and building for the past hour, impeding her vision as well as increasing her fear.

She should have arrived at the main road by now. Caleb had told her his cabin was a little more than a mile in, but she was sure she'd walked at least two. She could still hear the creek down below and had assumed that it followed the road to the highway.

She'd obviously assumed wrong.

The road must have turned somewhere. Split into another road. She'd have to backtrack and make her way to the highway quickly. She had no idea how far it would be back down the mountain and into the city, but she had to at least try before morning came.

Before Caleb discovered she was gone.

She didn't blame him, of course. If even a computer said she was married to Sam Phillips, then why would Caleb believe her, a woman who had obviously lost not only her memory, but her mind, as well?

The moon reappeared, throwing silvery light over the dirt road, and she hurried back the way she'd come. The air felt heavy and cold, and even though she wore jeans and boots and a borrowed denim jacket from Caleb, she couldn't stop from shaking.

She hated leaving without saying goodbye. He'd saved her life, taken care of her. But she knew that what she felt for Caleb was much more than gratitude. Even when he'd kissed her, and she'd certainly kissed him back, she'd denied her feelings. But when he'd told her he was taking her back to Phillips, she couldn't deny the truth any longer.

She'd fallen in love with Caleb.

She knew it was insane. Falling in love with a man she hardly knew. One more thing to prove she was "mentally unstable," as Phillips had told Caleb.

But whatever her feelings were for Caleb, she had no intention of going anywhere with Sam Phillips, even if she was married to the man. She was going to fight this. Alone, if she had to. Once she got to the city, maybe she would remember something, some little thing that might help her sort this out.

She jumped at the sound of an owl hooting close by. The moon had disappeared again, and the blackness made it impossible to see. Leaves rustled behind her, and the snap of a twig made her freeze.

*Stay calm, stay calm,* she repeated over and over, but she barely heard herself over the pounding of her heart. Slowly she backed to the edge of the road. The swollen creek rushed in the blackness below her. Another snap of a twig. The moon reappeared in time to catch the shadow of a dark, thick form moving straight at her. She screamed and stumbled backward, over the edge.

She caught the branch of a bush, struggled to hold on. The creek rose in the blackness below her like the open jaws of a great monster. Above her the dark form closed in.

The branch snapped off, and she cried out as she slid down another foot before grabbing on to a rock. Her boots slipped in the damp earth, and she heard the sound of rocks and dirt falling into the water below.

*"Don't let her get away, dammit! Kill her if you have to, but don't let her get away."* Rain pelted her, lightning flashed, illuminating the man's face above her. It was the devil himself, with angry dark eyes. He

*grabbed her arms, pulled her toward him...she struck
out at him...*

*She fell...*

"Sarah!"

She fought against the hands that held her, struggled with every ounce of strength she had, but he was
too strong, too determined. He pulled her upward,
away from the creek and rocks below. Desperate, she
lunged at him and sank her teeth into his knuckles.

"Sarah, dammit, stop! It's me, Caleb!"

*Caleb?*

She released her hold. Caleb? Confused, she went
limp, then felt his strong, warm body against hers as
he pulled her into his arms. They tumbled back onto
the road together. She cried out again as Wolf barked,
then licked her face. The animal reluctantly obeyed
when Caleb ordered him to sit.

"What in the hell were you thinking?" he said raggedly, dragging her closer to him. His breathing
matched hers, hard and heavy. She rested her forehead against his chest, felt the pounding of his heart.

"You can't take me to that man," she gasped between breaths.

"I won't." He held her closer.

Relief poured through her. She burrowed her face
against his neck, drawing strength from his masculine
scent.

"Sarah, we've got to get back to the cabin. It's going to rain."

She shook her head and twisted her fingers into the
lapels of his jacket. "Caleb, you've got to listen to
me."

"I won't take you to him," he repeated. "You have my word."

"No, you don't understand." She pulled away from him. "My memory, who I am," she said, her voice shaking. "I remember. I remember everything."

# Six

"My name is Sarah Jane Grayson. I'm twenty-six years old, and I'm a librarian at the Los Angeles County Library. I live at 5234 Bedford in Valencia and I drive a blue Honda."

Rain hammered on the roof, and an occasional crack of thunder shook the walls. They'd been caught in the initial downpour and had been soaking wet by the time they'd gotten back to the cabin. Sarah had changed into her skirt and one of Caleb's white shirts, and he'd put on dry jeans and a flannel shirt. Sitting by the fire now, with Caleb beside her, Sarah felt safer than she had in a very long time.

"Several days ago," she went on, "three FBI agents came to my apartment, asking about a friend of mine, Robert Burke, an art journalist I dated and often helped with research at the library. Robert was killed three weeks ago—a hit-and-run accident. Or at least I thought it was an accident. Now I'm not so sure."

Caleb handed her a glass of whiskey. She took a sip, then coughed as the liquid burned a fiery trail down her throat. "I don't usually drink," she gasped.

He raised a brow. "You don't say."

She smiled. "My grandmother didn't approve of the spirits…in any form. You were right, by the way. I was raised in South Carolina until I was eleven, and my family moved to California. My parents were killed in a car accident when I was fourteen, and I went to live with my grandmother, but Granny got sick shortly after that, and I took care of her until she passed away six months ago. I moved into a small house of my own and felt like a little kid again, scared and excited all at the same time. I even bought a bottle of champagne, though I'm sure Granny turned over in her grave because of it."

Caleb shook his head. "Quite the rebel, aren't you?"

Sarah knew he was making fun of her, but she was so happy to have her memory back, to have a name and a past, she didn't care. "As a matter of fact—" she lifted her chin "—I drank half the bottle."

His expression was dubious. "And?"

"And I was sick all night, of course."

He took the glass from her and set it on the hearth. "Tell me about the agents."

She nodded grimly. "They wanted me to come in for questioning. The one who did all the talking was Howard, Special Agent Victor Howard. Tall, short blond hair, maybe around forty."

"That's our man," Caleb said tightly.

"He wanted to talk to me about Robert. I told him I was leaving in the morning for Mexico. After Robert's death, I realized how uncertain life really is and I decided to do something daring and go on an exotic vacation by myself. It was my first real vacation since Granny had taken ill. Actually, it was the *only* vacation I'd ever planned. My bags were packed, I'd rented a little house on the beach in Puerto Vallarta. I'd even bought my first bikini." She laughed at herself, then looked away. "A real woman of the world, huh?"

Caleb knew there were women who selflessly gave up their own lives, sacrificed their own wants and needs for loved ones; he'd just never met one. For the first time in his life he felt truly humbled.

"Agent Howard was insistent," she said, continuing. "He assured me he'd have me back in time to get a good night's sleep, and I couldn't very well say no to the FBI, could I?"

*Sure you could,* Caleb thought. He'd done it dozens of times. But he also understood how easy it was to intimidate a civilian. Especially a young, single female. He wasn't exactly proud of it, but he'd done it himself more than once. If Howard had wanted to bring her in, there was nothing Sarah could have done to stop him.

"What happened then?" he asked.

"He said we were going to his headquarters so he could take an official statement, but he just kept driving. When he turned off into the mountains, I questioned him, but he just smiled and said that his division in the FBI had an office up there."

A flash of lightning illuminated the cabin, and a roll of thunder rattled the windows. Sarah jumped, and instinctively Caleb slipped a hand over her shoulders. She drew in a sharp breath and relaxed again.

"It started to rain hard," she said, her voice strained and quiet. "Agent Howard was driving, and I was in the front seat with him. The other two agents were in the back seat. It was creepy. The bigger one, with straight brown hair and squinty eyes, he frightened me the most, but neither one of them ever said a word, they just stared at me. There was something in their eyes, something in the way they were looking at me, as if they knew some secret about me that pleased them."

*They were going to kill her.* He'd seen that look in a man's eye before, he knew that some men took great pleasure in taking a life, the more vulnerable the victim, the better they liked it. No doubt they'd had something else planned for her, too, Caleb thought grimly, before they killed her. A rage built slowly in him, curling up from inside him like the flames from hell.

"Caleb," she said, wincing. "You're hurting me."

He suddenly realized he'd tightened his hold on the back of her neck. Cursing, he released her, then lightly ran his fingers over the delicate skin he'd nearly bruised. Trusting, she leaned into his touch and he resolved he'd save his anger for later. When Sarah was safe and out of the way, there would be retribution. Agent Victor Howard and his buddies could count on that.

"Go on," he said, brushing her hair away from her shoulders.

"There was an explosion, like a gunshot, and the car swerved. It was a flat tire. The two men in the back got out, but Agent Howard stayed with me, started asking me questions about Robert, how well I knew

him, if I'd worked with him. When I told him that
Robert and I were just good friends and I helped him
occasionally with his research, he seemed very interested, anxious even. He wanted to know exactly what
kind of research, if I kept files or copies of computer
disks that he could look at for his investigation.''

"What kind of investigation?''

She shook her head. "I don't know. But I told him
Robert and I worked on a lot of different things, and
that Robert always kept his own files and disks, even
when he used the library computers. The library
doesn't store users' files for more than a few days.
Agent Howard seemed angry at my answer.''

Thunder shook the cabin again, and Sarah hugged
her arms around her. Wolf rose from his spot by the
front door, whining softly as he began to pace.

"It was the same that night,'' she said softly, staring into the fire. "Lightning and thunder and pour-
ing rain. I could hear the men outside swearing as they
worked on the tire. Agent Howard wasn't smiling
anymore, didn't even pretend to be friendly. His voice
got louder, he kept insisting that I knew something. It
was dark, but I could still see the look in his eyes, the
fury that I didn't know anything. I think that's when
I realized there was no FBI office in the mountains,
and that I was probably never going to wear that bikini I'd bought.''

Caleb pulled Sarah into his arms and waited for her
shaking to ease. She nestled against his chest, her
breathing ragged and warm.

"Howard got out of the car then and started to yell
at the men to hurry up. He said that the ladies were
waiting and time was running out.''

"What ladies?'' Caleb asked.

She shook her head. "I don't know, but they started to argue then, about me, about 'just getting it over with,' one of them said. They must not have thought I could hear them, or else they just didn't care. Caleb—" she lifted her head and looked into his eyes "—they wanted to kill me. *Me,* of all people, a simple, nothing little librarian."

He wanted to tell her she was anything but simple, and that she sure as hell wasn't "nothing." It scared him just how much she was, and how much she meant. "Tell me what happened."

"I got out of the car, thinking I might slip away in the dark. One of them saw me and yelled. Howard told them to go after me. 'Kill her if you have to,' he said, 'but don't let her get away.'"

*Bastards!* Caleb's insides twisted with rage, but he forced himself to remain calm. He needed to know everything, every detail. It would be to his advantage when he went after Howard.

Sarah drew in a long, shuddering breath. "I ran, then slipped in the mud. One of the men, the larger one with squinty eyes, he grabbed me from behind. Luther, I heard Howard call him. That's the one I bit, then kicked. He went down, but Howard and the other one were right there. I backed toward the cliff, lost my footing and started to slip down. Howard grabbed me, but I broke away and fell down into the darkness. I don't remember anything after that."

"Not even me finding you?"

"No," she said wearily. "Caleb, what could they possibly want from me?"

"You know something, Sarah," he said. "Whether you realize it or not, you either saw or heard something, or have access to information Howard needs. It obviously has something to do with your friend. Whatever it is, it has to be important and a threat to Howard. Otherwise he never would take the chances he's taking to get to you.''

"But how can he change computer files like that, create a person that doesn't exist? That's dishonest.''

It amazed him there truly was a person as naive as Sarah. Her innocence brought out every protective instinct within him. He wondered what she'd think of him if she knew even a small part of the things he'd done. Things that were a hell of a lot worse than changing a computer file.

"An FBI agent, any government agency, for that matter, has access to every computer entry ever made about you,'' Caleb explained, "no matter how private. He also has the ability to change those files to say anything he wants.''

"But to say he's my *husband!* Who would ever believe that?''

He said nothing, just looked down at her wide baby blue eyes. She stiffened and pulled back.

"*You* believed it,'' she whispered.

He nodded stiffly. "For a while. And that's all Howard needs. A little time. If he'd found you, he would have had you away from here before anyone could question anything. Like you said, who would say no to the FBI?''

She stared at him oddly for a moment. "You sound as if you know, as if you're familiar with this sort of subterfuge.''

He could tell her that he was not only familiar with it, but that he'd helped write the book. Somehow he didn't think this was a good time to share that little bit of news. For that matter, she never needed to know.

Once he had her in a safe place, he could take care of Howard. After that, she could go back to her life. To Mexico. She could wear that bikini she'd bought and forget any of this ever happened.

The question was, could he?

"It's common knowledge the government can go anywhere and do whatever they want," he said evasively. "Especially if they don't get caught. Whatever it is that Howard is up to, he doesn't expect to get caught."

Sarah's shoulders slumped heavily. "He'll be back, won't he?"

*He'll be back,* Caleb thought, *but I'll be ready for him.* He slipped his index finger under her chin and forced her to look at him. "You're safe for now. I won't let him near you."

"I know," she said quietly.

She held his gaze. He saw the trust in her eyes, the acceptance. No one had ever looked at him like that before. The feel of her skin under his fingers made him ache, made him want things he didn't know he was capable of wanting. He dropped his hand away.

"You have to do everything I tell you," he said tightly. "No more running away."

She stared at the hands she'd folded in her lap and nodded. "I—I'm sorry. I couldn't stand the thought of you handing me over to that man." She looked up at him, and he saw the sparkle of tears in her eyes. "Would you have?" she asked in a whisper. "Would you have given me to him?"

He met her steady gaze, felt his own blood pulse through his veins. He heard the pounding of the rain and the rumble of distant thunder.

"No."

Sarah felt her heart soar at Caleb's answer. She'd needed to know. In spite of everything that had happened, and no matter what was to come, she had to know. His single word skimmed over her like a comforting hand. Her throat felt thick with relief. "Thank you."

"I'm going to call a friend of mine. He'll be able to...take care of you better than I can. You'll be safer with him."

She couldn't imagine feeling safer with anyone other than Caleb. Her heart, which had felt so light only a moment before, grew heavy. And though the fire warmed her, she felt suddenly cold inside. She knew she couldn't stay here. It was foolish of her to think that she could. Or that he would want her to.

And why would he? It was obvious that Caleb was a man of experience. With women, with the world. She was a sheltered, naive librarian who'd foolishly fallen in love with a man who wouldn't have looked twice at her if he hadn't been forced to.

"When?" she asked quietly. "When will I have to leave?"

"In the morning, early. I'll have to make a phone call, then get you out of here before Howard retraces his steps and comes back."

"In the morning," she repeated softly. She lifted her gaze to Caleb's. His jaw was set rigid, his mouth hard and thin. She could still smell the storm on him and his own masculine scent that made her pulse race. She might never see him again, she realized.

*What the hell,* she thought, taking a deep breath. She'd already made a fool out of herself. Why not go all the way?

Her fingers were shaking as she reached out and laid a hand on his chest. "Well, then," she said and heard the tremble in her voice, "we just have tonight, don't we?"

He went still at her words. It seemed as if the very room had stilled. She no longer heard the pounding of the rain, only the pounding of her pulse and the feel of Caleb's heavy heartbeat under her fingertips. "Sarah—"

She pressed her fingers to his lips. "No, Caleb, don't say it. For just a little while, in the time we have left, I want to pretend that none of this happened. That there are no agents out there and no one's after me. I want to pretend it's just you and me."

His hand circled the wrist she still had on his chest, but he didn't move it. She felt the tension course from his body into hers, understood that he was struggling to maintain control, control that she was equally determined to break down.

But how? She'd never seduced a man before. She had no idea how to make a man want her, certainly not a man like Caleb. She decided to let instinct take over, to just do what felt right.

She drew in a slow, shaky breath. "Make love to me."

His entire body stiffened, and the dark intensity of his eyes sent a flood of liquid heat racing through her.

"You don't know what you're asking," he said, his voice oddly strained.

"That's exactly why I'm asking." She traced his lips with her fingertips, remembered what they'd felt like covering her own. "I want to know. I want you to show me."

He didn't move, didn't speak, and she was certain she'd lost the battle. Good Lord, she could hardly force the man! Tears built in her eyes as she slowly pulled away from him.

"You don't want me," she said blankly. "I-I'm sorry. I've put you in an awkward situation... again."

*Not want her?* Caleb found it impossible to speak, he wanted her so badly. When he'd found her gone earlier, he nearly went crazy. The thought of her alone out in the woods, where she might have been hurt, had sent him into a frenzy. People were lost in the mountains all the time, sometimes they were never found. If it hadn't been for Wolf, he might never have found her.

Or Victor Howard might have.

He'd known earlier, before he'd discovered Sarah missing, that he couldn't have handed her over to the man. He would have turned over every stone, followed every lead to verify his story before he would have let Sarah go with him. Even then, he didn't know if he could have. And though he was glad that he didn't have to now, he still knew there was no place in his life for her, either. It would be like jumping from the proverbial frying pan into the fire.

A man with his job could never have a wife or children. They would be the first target for anyone who wanted to get to him, and there was always someone who wanted to get to him. The danger was too great. He sure as hell hadn't saved her once so that he could be the one who eventually caused her death.

It was too late for him to change his life, but not Sarah. There were so many things for her still to see and do. He thought of those things, the places he could show her.... No. He'd send her with Mike tomorrow, get her far away from here. Far away from him.

*Then we just have tonight, don't we...*

Her words had sent his heart hammering and his pulse pounding in his temple. He looked at her now, saw the flush of color on her delicate cheekbones and the hurt in her big blue eyes. Her skin glowed in the light of the fire, skin that was softer than rose petals. Golden sparks danced in her hair. Unable to resist, he tucked a loose strand behind her ear, then watched her intake of breath as he ran his fingertips over her earlobe and down her neck.

*Not want her?* He wanted her so much he found it difficult to breathe. "Sarah," he said, "you've been through a lot. You're confused right now. Things will look different in the morning."

She rubbed her cheek against the palm of his hand. "I see things more clearly than ever, perhaps than I ever have. Victor Howard almost killed me, Caleb. I would have died if it hadn't been for you."

His fingers stilled. "Is that what this is about? Gratitude?"

She shook her head. "What I'm saying is that life has a different meaning to me now. Every moment is important, is precious to me. And right now, being here with you is more important and more precious than any moment in my entire life. I know I'm not very good at this," she said quietly. "Nor will I pretend to be. But I want to be here, with you, even if it's just for tonight."

*Not very good at this?* Good Lord, he thought with a quiet groan, if she were any better, he wouldn't know his own name. Her innocence, her lack of guile, excited him more than any other woman had even come close to.

"You really don't know how beautiful you are, do you?" he said, cupping her chin in his hand. Her pale, porcelain-like skin against his tanned, callused hand heightened his awareness of their differences. Differences that aroused him fully, to the point of pain.

Embarrassed by his compliment, she lowered her gaze demurely. He watched the firelight play over her delicate features and light up the silver and gold in her hair. His insides tightened. God, how he wanted her. Like he'd never wanted before.

And then she lifted her gaze to him. The innocence in her eyes was gone, in its place a bold, seductive look that made his heart stop. She leaned closer and the scent of her, the scent that he'd come to recognize as hers alone, settled over him like a net spun of silken threads.

"Make love to me, Caleb," she whispered. "Please."

Her soft plea snapped the last of his control. On an oath, he pulled her to him, dragging his hand through her hair and tilting her head back. Her eyes darkened to a smoky blue, and he held her sensuous gaze, drinking in the incredibly erotic sight of her. Her lips parted, inviting him, tempting him....

He covered her mouth with his.

All rational thought left him. He felt the same wildly urgent need move from her body into his as she answered his kiss. Her breasts pressed against his chest. He ached to touch them, to draw each hardened nipple into his mouth, to taste every inch of her, but he wanted to go slowly with her, to savor every moment with her, because he knew it would have to last a lifetime.

Her arms slid around his neck, pulling him closer, and he heard her soft sigh of pleasure. He deepened the kiss, slanting his mouth, moving against her lips in a rhythm as old as time. She responded eagerly, meeting every hot thrust of his tongue with her own. And when her hips began to move with the same rhythm, he lost his last thread of control.

With the rain outside and the fire beside them, they sank to the floor, aware only of each other. He laid her on the rug in front of the fireplace, easing his weight carefully over hers. Blood pounded in his temples and raced through his body until he thought he might explode from the force.

He dragged his mouth from hers and rained kisses over her neck. She arched toward him with a whimper, then gasped as he traced his tongue over the velvet curve of her earlobe.

"Caleb," she breathed his name heavily, "there is one more thing. Something I'd forgotten, that I remembered tonight. I think you should know."

He moved down her neck, delighting in the way she responded to the slightest touch from him. "Hmm," he answered, but truly wasn't listening.

"I—" she sighed as his mouth moved lower and his hand moved upward "—I'm a virgin."

# Seven

Caleb suddenly went very still. Sarah watched as he slowly lifted his head and looked at her. Her heart beat furiously, not only from his touch, but from the fear of his response to her declaration. She saw the passion in his eyes, marveled that she was actually responsible for it, but the control in him she'd felt slip only moments ago was back again.

He drew in a long breath and rose on one elbow to gaze down at her. "Sarah," he said carefully, "you're twenty-six years old."

She nodded.

"And the man who was killed, Robert, you said he was your boyfriend."

"I said he was my friend. Agent Howard thought he was my boyfriend, but Robert didn't—" she felt her cheeks burn "—well . . . we were just friends."

He continued to stare at her, a mixture of amazement and desire and uncertainty on his face. "You mean to tell me you never, that you haven't—"

She shook her head. "I dated a little, but I just never met the right man. And the few dates I did go on turned into wrestling matches, so I wasn't exactly enthusiastic to go out much. I liked dating Robert, he never put those pressures on me. I felt safe." She looked away. "I'd always planned to, but I was so busy with work and Granny and it just never happened."

Caleb rolled his eyes. "Dammit, Sarah. It's not like taking a trip or enrolling in a class."

"For me it was," she said with a sigh. "Of course, I dreamed about it, like every other woman, that I'd be swept off my feet and carried away to a castle where we'd live happily ever after and make lots of babies, but I knew that would never happen to me."

Caleb's mouth thinned. "It can still happen. Twenty-six is not exactly doddering, for God's sake."

She should have felt humiliated, talking about herself like this with a man. And yet she didn't. She looked at him, then reached up and slid her fingers through his thick hair. His jaw clenched at her gentle touch.

"Caleb, I've gone through too much with you to be embarrassed about who I am. There's no undoing the past—nor do I want to—but this is the present. Right now. And whatever future I may have, I want to remember this night and being with you."

His fingers circled her wrist and tightened. He did not move her hand away, nor did he pull her closer. He stared at her for what seemed like an eternity, his look that of a man standing on a train trestle facing an oncoming train. Did he jump a hundred feet down, or did he face the train?

Lightning flashed, and the room burst alive with silvery light. Thunder growled. Overhead the rain beat a steady rhythm. She watched his face, the play of the fire and the lightning over the rugged angles of his square jaw and dark eyes. His black gaze burned her.

"There are no castles. No 'happily ever after,' and no babies. Not here, not with me. Can you face that tomorrow?"

If she could face losing Caleb, then she could face anything. "I want you." She reached up and touched his cheek, then lifted her body closer to his. "More than I've ever wanted anything in my entire life."

She brought her lips closer to his, felt him stiffen. Disappointment and fear made her hesitate. If he rejected her now, left her wanting like this, how would she ever handle it? Desperation drove her on, determination and instinct led the way. "Kiss me," she whispered. "Make love to me."

His fingers tightened painfully on her wrist; his eyes narrowed. A groan rose from deep in his throat; low and guttural, a wild, animal-like sound that made her heart slam against her chest.

He moved so fast then, dragging her against him, covering her mouth with his, it was impossible to think. Desire exploded through her, and all she could do was feel. Sensation after sensation poured through her, heat and light and color; a swirling kaleidoscope of sights and sounds and smells, every one of them Caleb. The pleasure she'd felt only moments ago turned to sheer, aching need. She wound her arms around his neck, giving herself up to the feel and taste of him.

She arched into him, wanting him closer, *needing* him closer. She felt weak yet powerful at the same time. A power that no man had ever shown her before, a power she would never know again. There was only Caleb. That's all there ever would be.

The rug pressed against her back, and he lay beside her, his long, muscular body like a taut bow over hers. His mouth moved over hers, hot as liquid fire, and the flames spread through her as if she were dry kindling. He kissed her relentlessly, moving over her face, her ear, her neck, then lower still. He released the top buttons of the shirt she wore—*his* shirt—and his fingertips caressed the soft rise of her breast. Impatient, she worked at the buttons of his shirt and pushed the fabric out of her way, then ran her hands restlessly over his chest. His muscles bunched with tension, and the coarse feel of his hair against her smooth fingertips heightened her awareness of him and excited her at the same time.

She lowered her mouth to the skin under her hands. It was hot, slightly salty and incredibly male. And when she tentatively touched her tongue to the circle surrounding his nipple, he sucked in a sharp breath.

"Sarah—" his voice was thick "—you positive you've never done this before?"

She rubbed her cheek against his chest and smiled. "I'm sure I would have remembered."

And Caleb knew he'd never forget. Her touch, her amazingly soft body, her sweet, feminine scent. A hunger he'd never dreamed possible built inside him, so strong, so intense, it nearly had him drawing back. He'd asked her if she could face the morning, but could he?

And then she touched him again and all coherent thought was gone.

With a growl, he tucked her beneath him, struggling to hold on to the last thread of control. He didn't want to frighten her; the thought that he might hurt her scared the hell out of him. "Sarah," he said hesitantly, "this is a first for me, too."

She stared at him though passion-filled eyes. As his words sank in, confusion knotted her brow. "You've never done this before?"

In spite of himself, he smiled. "I've done *this* before. What I mean is, I've never been with a, that is, I never—"

"Made love to a virgin?" she finished for him.

"No." Why did Caleb have the feeling the roles were suddenly reversed? That she was the one teaching him? An awkwardness he hadn't felt since he was a teenager crept over him. "I'm not sure how it will be for you."

"Caleb," she murmured, "there are some things a woman knows, not only with her mind and body, but with her heart." She touched his cheeks with her fingertips and held his worried gaze. "And *I* know. With all my heart, I know it will be wonderful."

"I don't want to hurt you." He covered her hand with his own. "God knows, I don't want to hurt you."

"You won't."

She pulled him to her, parting her lips with a sigh as he gently kissed her. A longing tore through him he'd never felt before, a need that went far beyond the physical. *Another first,* he realized in stunned amazement.

He tasted the whiskey she'd sipped only minutes ago, and the warm, sweet thrust of her tongue sent his blood pulsing through his veins. Her hands moved over his shoulders and neck, then through his hair, and the touch of her fingers over his scalp sent a wave of pleasure through him. Never had a woman made him feel like this before; no fantasy or dream could have come close. He moved to the curve of her jaw, the hollow of her throat. He touched her pulse there with his tongue, felt the erratic beat of her heart. His own heart hammered against his ribs, a primitive, wild rhythm of life. She was his, if only for the moment, for the night, she belonged to him.

Sarah rejoiced in each new sensation, every nuance. Her body sang an unfamiliar tune with a clarity and depth that stunned her. She felt shaky and hot, and it seemed as if the storm had moved into the room, into their bodies. They were all one, part of each other, a melding of nature and man, of man and woman. She shuddered with the power that coursed through her, the energy, the need to fill and be filled.

She moved beneath him, anxious, impatient, desperately wanting his hands on her body, on her skin. His lips moved over her; the light scrape of his chin on her neck sent tiny electric currents shimmering through her. Her breathing grew heavy and fast, and a yearning from somewhere deep inside of her increased to a sharp ache.

"Touch me," she murmured, certain that if he didn't, she would surely die.

"I intend to, sweetheart."

Suddenly he straightened, rising to his knees and pulling her with him. She gasped at the unexpected move, but before she could utter a protest, he dragged her mouth to his and kissed her roughly. Her head swam and her bones felt as if they were melting. She swayed when he pulled away again and looked down at her.

Desire darkened his eyes as he unfastened her top button. Her breath caught as his fingertips brushed over her sensitive skin. She wanted to help him, but found she couldn't lift her arms. He moved slowly from button to button, deliberately, and the anticipation heightened her excitement. Her breasts grew tight and heavy.

The blouse slipped off her shoulders, and with a quick flick of his fingers, he removed her bra. The cool air slid over her naked skin. He was staring at her, the hard, angular lines of his face defined in the firelight.

No man had ever looked at her this way, with such raw, open passion. She became fully aware of how large he was beside her, how vulnerable she was, yet she wasn't frightened. His masculinity only heightened her own sense of femininity, and she felt a power she'd never dreamed possible.

She wanted to know everything, to experience a lifetime in one night. She hadn't time to be shy or coy, every minute was as precious to her as her next breath. She reached out to him, took his hands in hers, then guided them to her breasts. She heard his intake of breath, felt the shudder that passed from his body into hers. And when he lowered his head to her and his lips moved over the curve of her soft flesh, she moaned.

It wasn't possible to feel such pleasure, she thought dimly. But it was, and she did. His mouth closed over her hardened nipple, and his tongue, hot and wet, circled the pearled tip. Pleasure exploded inside her, and she arched toward him, raking her hands through his hair as she cried out. He cupped her buttocks in his hands, nearly lifting her off the floor. She clung to him, gasping for breath as his mouth worked magic on her, making everything outside the two of them disappear.

A blissful, exquisite ache swept through her, centering between her legs. It wasn't enough. She wanted, *needed* more. She ran her hands over the hard, muscled planes of his arms. His skin was hot and damp under her fingertips. When she moved her hands lower, reaching for the snap of his jeans, he jumped.

"Did I do something wrong?" she asked, pulling her hand away.

"Ah, sweetheart, no." He lightly brushed his cheek over her breast, and the sensation of his beginning beard sent off sparks inside her. "You are right on...*so* right..."

He straightened then and lifted her body to his. The fire lit their bodies and they knelt, torso to torso, bare skin to bare skin. Sarah sighed her pleasure at the contact, and yet it *still* wasn't enough. She leaned closer, circling his neck with her arms, and felt the hard proof of his arousal pressing at the juncture of her thighs, exactly where the tension coiling inside her had centered. She moved against him instinctively, with a rhythm as old as time. He groaned deeply.

He moved so quickly it was a blur, and suddenly she was on her back again. He knelt over her, his breathing ragged, his eyes fierce. His hand moved to the snap on his jeans. She heard the soft hiss of a zipper.

"Caleb," she whispered his name, beckoning him. Golden light shimmered on his damp skin. Fire burned in his gaze.

The sound of his name on her lips nearly sent Caleb over the edge. He felt a hunger so intense, so powerful, he had to clench his fists to regain control. And though he desperately wanted to take her now, to drive himself into her, hard and fast, he knew he couldn't. With a restraint he couldn't have imagined he possessed, he drew in a shaky breath and loosened his hands.

She lay like a goddess in front of him, the firelight dancing on her flushed, bare skin. Her soft breasts rose and fell with her shallow breathing, and her hair, fanned around her face, came alive with sparks of red and gold and silver.

"You *are* beautiful," he said, his voice husky and thick.

She smiled shyly and looked away.

"No," he whispered. "Look at me."

She lifted her gaze to him again, her blue eyes shining. He bent over her and pressed his lips lightly to her, then slid his hand down slowly, gently cupping each breast before moving down to the zipper on her skirt. He could have simply lifted the fabric and entered her, but he wanted her naked beneath him. In one fluid movement, the skirt was gone.

Her legs were long and slender, and he ached to have them wrapped tightly around him. He slid his hand over the curve of her hip, then dipped his fingers under the waistband of her panties, tugging them out of the way. He looked down at her long, sleek body, and pleasure pounded through him like the heavy beat of a drum.

He bent over her, kissing her lips, her chin, then nuzzling one soft breast. He slowly moved his hand between her legs, opening her to him while he ca-

ressed the sensitive flesh with his finger. Sarah gasped
and arched upward, calling his name sharply.

"Relax," he crooned, stroking her as he tested her
body's barrier. She moved against him, nearly cry-
ing. She was hot and moist and tight, and just the incredible feel of her was more than he could stand.

He couldn't wait any longer. He moved quickly,
peeling off his jeans, then positioning himself over her.
Their eyes met. "I'll stop anytime you say," he said
raggedly. "It might kill me, but I'll do it."

"If you stop, *I'll* kill you," she said fiercely.

He smiled, then eased himself into her.

Lightning flashed, illuminating the room, thunder
shook the roof. Sarah saw the fierce, wild expression
on Caleb's face as he entered her. Sweat creased his
brow, and his muscles bunched tightly. An urgent,
driving need consumed her. She wrapped her arms and
legs around him and surged upward, meeting his body
with hers.

The pain lasted only a moment. Pleasure rushed in
quickly to take its place as he moved deeper within her.
She cried, not from the momentary pain, but from
sheer joy. He kissed her tears and her cheeks and
whispered to her, but she was too overcome with
emotion to understand what he said.

He moved slowly, gently, and the tension built to a
fever pitch. She met him with every move, with every
kiss, the urgency like a living thing inside her. She
heard him groan when she ran her hands down his
back and over his firm buttocks. It amazed her that
her touch created the same response in him that his did
to her. She moved her hands eagerly over him, exploring every valley, every angle of his tightly muscled body, delighting in the reaction her touch elicited.

He grew harder inside her, larger, and she moaned in ecstasy, lifting her hips madly against his. The tension grew, tighter and tighter, higher and faster...

"Caleb!"

Her senses exploded and she clung to him, sobbing his name. He thrust deeply, moving faster, until she felt his own body stiffen and convulse. He groaned, then pulled her tightly against him and buried his face in her neck.

It was impossible to speak, so they listened to the sound of their hearts beating and the rhythm of the rain.

She lay cradled in his arms for what seemed like a long time, but perhaps it was only minutes. As her skin began to cool, she shivered. Caleb reached for the woolen throw blanket on the couch and settled it over them, wrapping them up in a cocoon of warmth.

She wanted to thank him, but the words seemed childish and inadequate for what had just happened. Making love had answered so many questions; it had unlocked mysteries and transformed fantasy into reality. She felt enlightened, alive.

She felt like a woman.

And he certainly felt like a man. Amazed at her boldness, she ran her fingers down his broad chest and over his muscled thigh. He sucked in a sharp breath at her touch, then circled her waist with his arm and hauled her against him.

"You're amazing," he said, nuzzling her earlobe.

"Me?" She shivered at the erotic slide of his tongue over her ear. "What did I do?"

"You really don't know, do you?"

She shook her head. "Tell me."

He lifted his head and looked into her eyes. "I've never met anyone like you. Not in my entire life."

She frowned. "That's not necessarily good."

"It's good." He pressed his lips to her shoulder. "Better than good, Sarah. A hell of a lot better."

Warmed by his compliment, she snuggled closer. "You're good, too."

He raised one eyebrow. "Good, huh?"

"Better than good," she whispered. "A hell of a lot better."

He chuckled. "You're a vamp, Sarah Jane Grayson. A dangerous woman."

*Dangerous?* She delighted in his description of her, ridiculous as it was. She was hardly a woman of the world, but with Caleb, she almost believed it. For this one night, she *would* believe it.

And deep down, she knew that she *was* changed forever. She would never be the same Sarah Jane Grayson again. Nothing would look the same, feel or sound the same again.

With a sigh, she slid her hands through his hair and pulled his lips to hers, kissing him with all the passion he'd awakened in her. She felt him grow harder, and she marveled at her ability to evoke such a response.

Tomorrow she knew she would leave him, that she might never see him again. But there was tonight, this moment, and she intended to live minute by minute, heartbeat by heartbeat, whisper by whisper.

Jaw set tight, hands white knuckled, Caleb gripped the steering wheel of his Jeep and nearly flew over the dirt road leading in to the cabin. The storm had moved on during the night, but a few puddles of water remained in the numerous ruts dotting the road. He splashed through each one, spewing water and mud in his wake.

He'd been gone too long, dammit. He glanced at his watch and cursed again. Ten o'clock. He'd intended to be back by nine and have Sarah out of here, but his phone call to Mike had taken longer than he'd expected, and on his way back, Mrs. Wells, the fourth- and fifth-grade teacher, had been stranded on the side of the road outside of town with a flat tire. He could hardly have left her there, but changing the tire had cost him precious time.

Still, he had no reason to be concerned. He'd tracked down Howard and his men first thing when he'd come into town, and they'd been having breakfast at the café. When Caleb had made his call from a phone booth in front of the post office, Howard's truck had still been parked out front, and the men hadn't come out.

The name Victor Howard had rung all kinds of bells when Mike had pulled up his file in the computer. He was an agent all right. Twenty years with the FBI. His record was nothing exceptional, but he'd moved up the ranks by saying yes to the right superiors and stepping on anyone who got in his way, which, in Sarah's case, had included changing computer files and creating a fictitious business and identity. There were two charges by civilians of excessive force, both cases eventually dropped.

But Caleb still didn't know why Howard was after Sarah. The connection was undoubtedly Robert. The journalist had obviously stumbled onto something that Victor wanted kept quiet. Caleb was certain Victor had killed Robert to shut him up and then, worried that Sarah might know something, as well, Victor had gone after her. When she'd fallen over the cliff, Victor must have thought she'd died, but had found no body when he'd come back to double-check. He'd underestimated Sarah, Caleb thought with a grim smile, and no doubt the man was furious she'd gotten away. He wouldn't stop until he found her.

Caleb would kill the man with his bare hands before he would let him get close to her.

A rabbit darted in front of the truck, and Caleb swerved to avoid it. The Jeep went sideways, then straightened out. He forced his mind back to the road, knowing he couldn't afford any more lost time.

But it was impossible not to think of her. Of her long silken limbs intertwined with his, her soft sighs and throaty whispers. Or the way she trembled when he entered her. And he'd trembled, too. No woman had ever felt so right, had fitted him as she did. No woman had ever brought him beyond the physical, had made him want more. No woman ever would again.

In a crazy moment, he thought he would simply take her away. Go somewhere they'd never be found, where no one would ever know who they were. Maybe, just maybe, he could live like a normal man. In his perfect world he'd have a real house, an eight-to-five job, mow the lawn on Saturday. Practice making babies every night....

But there was no perfect world. Someone would find him, just as they'd found Tom and Jenny. The agency would call him in for "one more job," and that one job would cost Sarah her life.

And that was one chance he'd never take.

She didn't know what he did for a living. She didn't need to know. Once he took care of Howard, Sarah could go back to her life. She'd settle in and meet someone....

That thought ripped through him like a dull blade. That another man would touch her, make love to her, spend the rest of his life with her...

The road swam in front of him like a sea of red. He swore, blinking several times to clear his eyes. He had to stop thinking about her. Howard wasn't stupid, and Caleb knew he couldn't afford to make even one mistake, not with Sarah's life at stake.

A few more minutes, he thought, pulling up in front of the cabin. He'd have her out of here. Mike was sending someone he trusted to meet them outside of Pinewood. As soon as Sarah was safely away, he intended to confront Howard and his men by himself. His eyes narrowed with pleasure at the thought.

He cut the engine. Smoke drifted from the chimney, and in the distance he heard Wolf bark. Wet leaves squished under his boots as he hurried toward the front door. He cleared his mind, refusing to let the emotions overtake him. He had to let her go, he had no choice.

He threw open the front door, then kicked it shut behind him.

Her name died on his lips as the cold steel of a revolver dug into the back of his neck. He went rigid.

"Welcome, Mr. Hunter," Victor Howard said from his chair beside the fireplace. Sarah sat at his feet, her eyes red. "Your lovely 'bride' and I have been waiting for you. Please come in and join us."

# Eight

Sarah watched in horror as the man behind the door pulled Caleb's gun out of the waistband of his jeans, then shoved him into the middle of the room. She'd wanted to call out, to tell him to run, but Victor had promised a bullet in Caleb's head if she so much as whispered. The third man, Luther, the one whose hand she'd bitten, stood by the kitchen door. He stared at her now, his mouth set in a thin line as his fingers slid up and down the barrel of his gun.

"Phillips, wasn't it?" Caleb asked blandly.

"I think we can drop that pretense, don't you? Right along with your amusing newlywed story. Even the waitress at the café in town thought it unbelievable that the elusive Caleb Hunter had taken a bride."

"You were in town when I left," Caleb said, his tone heavy with boredom.

"You know what I really like about the people of Pinewood?" Victor smiled. "They're all so friendly. Especially that waitress. When I told her our engine wouldn't start and we were friends of yours, she actually loaned me her car. Imagine, a complete stranger."

"I'm sorry, Caleb." Tears burned Sarah's eyes. "I didn't hear them drive up or see the car."

Victor indicated the couch. "Why don't you have a seat, Mr. Hunter, and we'll talk."

"I'll stand."

Victor shrugged. "Suit yourself. I'm sure Frank and Luther won't mind, either. Moving targets are always more challenging." He ran his hand down Sarah's hair. "And you and Miss Grayson have certainly been a challenge. Surprisingly so."

Sarah stiffened at Victor's touch. A dangerous glint shone in Caleb's dark eyes as he stared at the man. He turned his gaze toward her, and she saw an imperceptible softening.

"You all right?" he asked.

She nodded. She'd been straightening the kitchen when they'd come in the back door. She hadn't even made it to the living room before she'd run straight into Luther.

"Of course she's all right. Well, other than this teensy little bruise here." Victor ran his fingers along her jaw and she flinched.

"I'm going to have to hurt you for that, Howard," Caleb said with quiet, deadly calm.

Unaffected by Caleb's threat, Victor smiled. "It was foolish of her to try and run. It only antagonized Luther here. I'm afraid he's still a little upset for that nasty little bite Miss Grayson bestowed on him the other night.''

''Oh, Luther,'' Caleb drawled, turning a hard smile at the man, ''by the way, how're the family jewels?''

Luther's mouth tightened, and he took a step forward.

*Stop it, Caleb!* Sarah screamed silently. Why was he antagonizing them? What could it possibly gain him, except a bullet?

''Now, now,'' Victor reprimanded. ''Let's all try to get along, for a few minutes, anyway. I have some questions I'd like answered, such as why Mr. Hunter here took a strange woman into his home and lied for her.'' He looked toward the bedroom with a fiendish grin. ''Unless, of course, he took her into more than his home.''

When Caleb didn't answer, the man by the front door stepped closer and swung his arm, hitting Caleb in the back of the head with the butt of his revolver. Caleb's head jerked, and he stumbled forward, but he still said nothing, just rubbed the back of his neck and stared silently at Victor. The man reached up to hit him again.

''No!'' Sarah cried. ''He found me. At the river. I was unconscious, and he brought me back here. When I woke up I had amnesia. I didn't even know my name.''

''Amnesia?'' Victor gave a bark of laughter. ''You expect me to believe that?''

''I don't give a damn what you believe,'' Caleb said, and the man hit him a second time. Caleb stumbled forward again, and this time when he touched his head, his fingers came away with blood.

"Stop it! Please!" She started to rise, to go to him, but Victor's fingers tightened painfully in her hair and jerked her back down.

"An interesting story." Victor kept his hand twisted in Sarah's hair and stared at Caleb. "But why didn't you take her to the police or a doctor?"

Caleb kept his hard, cold gaze locked on Victor. "She woke up for a few seconds when I first brought her back here, just long enough to convince me not to call anyone, that someone was trying to kill her. Imagine my surprise," Caleb said sarcastically, "to find out it was the FBI."

Victor glanced sharply at Sarah. "So I take it you remember now."

Sarah winced at the pressure Victor exerted on her scalp. Dammit! She wouldn't let this man beat her, to have her cowering like a helpless child. And even though her insides were shaking, she refused to let him know that she was afraid. She lifted her chin and looked at him. "Enough to put you away, *Agent* Howard. Permanently."

With a sigh Victor released her, then leaned forward in his chair and pulled on a pair of leather gloves. "Well, then, I suppose we haven't much time, have we? Sarah, dear, why don't you just tell me exactly what you know about Robert and the research he was working on at the time of his tragic death."

She felt an overwhelming desire to lunge at the man. "You killed him. Just like you tried to kill me."

Victor's face hardened. "Let's just stick to the questions. I asked you what you know about Robert's research."

She knew he was going to kill her, and Caleb, too, no matter what she said. The only thing she could hope for now was to buy a little time. She glanced at Caleb, saw the hard fury on his face. She loved him, and she'd do anything to save him, no matter what happened to her.

"All right," she said with a confidence she didn't feel. "I'll tell you what I know. On one condition."

"Condition?" Victor raised one brow. "I don't believe you have tremendous bargaining power at the moment, Miss Grayson."

She met his arrogant gaze. "You want me to help you, to be assured I'll give you the correct information, then you have to let Caleb go. Take me with you, back into Los Angeles, and I'll tell you what you want to know."

Caleb made a move toward her. "Sarah, don't—"

A sick knot twisted in Sarah's stomach as the man behind Caleb hit him again. With a grunt, Caleb went down on his knees beside the end table. Slowly he lifted his gaze to Victor. Sarah saw the rage there, the murderous intent, and knew if she didn't get out of here soon, they would kill him.

"Touching," Victor said. "It appears that Mr. Hunter does indeed care for Miss Grayson. Perhaps this will work out after all. You both behave yourselves, and just maybe you'll see each other again."

*No* maybe *about it,* Caleb thought, ignoring the pain swimming in his head as he drew in a slow, steadying breath. There was no way in hell he would ever let these men take Sarah. White-hot anger burned in his gut, anger directed not only at Howard, but at himself for so carelessly walking into a trap. He'd underestimated the man and how quickly he would move.

But then, Caleb realized, his eyes narrowing with cold satisfaction, Howard had also underestimated him.

Based on Howard's relaxed stance, it was obvious that the man considered him a backwards mountain man, a harmless bumpkin that could easily be controlled. The bastard behind the door was clumsy. If it had suited the situation, Caleb could have easily taken the man out at any time. With Sarah in the room, though, and Luther out of his reach, Caleb had no choice but to increase his odds.

So every time the man had hit him, Caleb had maneuvered himself closer to the end table.

The end table with the gun.

"He's lying, Sarah. He has to kill us both." Caleb braced himself on the table, inching his hand toward the drawer. "Don't go anywhere with him."

"You really should learn to trust people," Victor said, shaking his head. "Miss Grayson is perfectly safe with us. All she has to do is cooperate and we'll be eternally grateful."

*She'll be eternally dead,* Caleb thought. He watched Victor rise and offer his hand to Sarah. She ignored him and rose by herself, though he noted the slight sway as she stood.

"Caleb," she said, her voice strained, "I'm so sorry I got you into this. I don't know how to thank you ... for everything. I couldn't have—"

Luther grabbed her arm with bruising force and dragged her toward the front door. *Not yet,* Caleb told himself, though the sight of the man touching Sarah nearly made him lose control. Victor turned to Caleb as the man behind the door, Frank, reached for the doorknob. "I wouldn't recommend calling anyone,

Mr. Hunter. It might prove extremely hazardous to Miss Grayson's health.''

*Wait...*

Caleb watched the door open, felt the cold rush of air pour into the room. The drawer was no more than three inches from his reach....

Victor was turning away from Caleb when a black, snarling shape flew through the open doorway, connecting with Frank. The man fell backward, screaming. Luther held on to a struggling Sarah and pointed his gun at the entangled creature and man.

''Don't shoot,'' Victor yelled over the man's strangled cries and the furiously growling wolf. ''You'll hit Frank.''

*Now.*

''Sarah!'' Caleb had the drawer open and the gun in his hand as she looked at him. ''Get down!''

Victor dove for the floor as Luther swung his gun at Caleb.

''No!'' Sarah knocked Luther's arm upward. The gun discharged, and the bullet struck the ceiling. Plaster showered the room. Luther roared his fury, then shoved Sarah away from him, giving Caleb a clear shot, a shot that would have been fatal if Frank hadn't grabbed Luther's leg and pulled, screaming for help as he yanked the man off balance. Caleb fired as Luther went down on top of the wild animal and an hysterical Frank.

Caleb lunged for Sarah and dragged her toward the kitchen, firing into the living room behind them. Bullets exploded around them as they ducked through the kitchen and out the back door.

''Don't look back,'' he shouted as they ran for the trees. ''No matter what, keep running.''

Pain sliced through Caleb's head like a hot knife. He ignored it and kept on, pulling Sarah with him, forcing her to match his long strides.

"We can't leave Wolf," she cried.

"There's no choice."

Victor and his men shouted angrily behind them, and based on the sound, Caleb knew they were close. Too close.

It was too risky to backtrack to the Jeep, and the closest cabin was two miles away. Sarah would never last at this pace. Victor would overtake them in a matter of minutes. There was only one other place to go.

"This way." He veered sharply to the left and pulled Sarah with him.

Sarah's lungs were burning. She struggled for air, to keep up with Caleb, but the ground felt unsteady under her feet. Trees and bushes blurred together, branches slapped at her face as they ran.

She stumbled on a tree trunk and barely had time to regain her balance before Caleb dragged her on.

"I—I can't," she gasped.

"We're almost there." He tightened his hold. "It's right up ahead, on the other side of that crop of rocks."

What was he talking about? What was right up ahead? All she saw was forest, and all she heard was the sound of Victor's men closing in on them. They'd never make it. She couldn't run as fast as Caleb. She was holding them back.

"Caleb," she choked out, "leave me. I'll hide and you go for help."

"And miss all the fun?" They rounded the crop of rocks, and Caleb pulled her toward the thick undergrowth of bushes and shrubs that grew heavily around the base. "Not a chance, sweetheart."

They stopped suddenly. Her heart hammered against her chest and her sides ached. She couldn't go on, yet she knew if she didn't they were both dead.

Caleb buried his arm in one thick bush and spread the branches. Sarah gasped as he grabbed the back of her neck, shoved her down, then forward.

She fell into a cave.

It took her eyes a moment to adjust to the dim light inside. It wasn't a big cave, not quite tall enough to stand up in, but it appeared to be deep.

"Be still and wait for me," Caleb said quietly. "I'll be back."

She knelt and stared into the blackness at the back of the cave, praying that she hadn't invaded an animal's home. A shiver ran through her at the sound of heavy breathing, but she realized it was her own.

She'd had time to imagine every creepy-crawly from every nightmare she'd ever had by the time Caleb rejoined her. He adjusted the bushes in front of the entrance to the cave, nearly blocking out all light, then took hold of her arm and dragged her toward the back of the cave, which actually curved away from the entrance.

When his arms came around her, she fell against him and started to shake uncontrollably. She wanted to cry, but she didn't dare give in to that right now. If she did, she might not stop.

"They can't find us here," Caleb said, pulling her closer. "I made sure there are no tracks."

She felt the heavy beat of his heart and drew strength from the sound. "They won't give up, though, will they?"

"No. They can't afford to. He'll bring in more men, probably some dogs. All I could hope to do here is buy us a little time. Which reminds me—" he took hold of her arms and set her away from him "—what the hell were you doing back there? Why did you tell Victor you'd help him?"

It was too dark to see his face, but she heard the anger in his voice. But there was more than anger, she realized. There was concern.

And fear?

Had he come to care for her? she wondered. Really care for her? Not just a brave knight helping out a damsel in distress, but something more? Something that went beyond chivalry?

No. She couldn't let herself think that. Last night had been wonderful. He'd been gentle and passionate, but he'd never given her any indication that there was any future for them. Her emotions were simply on the edge right now. She couldn't think clearly. She was imagining how she *wanted* him to feel, not how he really felt.

"I couldn't let them kill you." Her voice shook with determination. "I had to tell them something, anything to give you some time."

He was quiet for a moment, then she felt his hands loosen on her shoulders. "Sarah, I can take care of myself. Don't take chances like that again."

She would take a hundred chances for him. A thousand. Didn't he realize that? Couldn't he see that she loved him? No, she realized, and the empty ache inside her increased. He didn't see. Because he didn't want to see. Because he didn't feel the same way.

She wouldn't think about that now. This wasn't the time or place. God willing, there would be a *later*. She would deal with her feelings then.

"Caleb—" she reached out and touched his cheek "—that man, Frank, he hit you so hard."

She couldn't see his smile, but she felt it. "I'm fine, but I would have loved to see the expression on that guy's face when Wolf flew at him. I owe that animal big-time."

"We both do." She silently prayed that the wolf had escaped unharmed.

Caleb's cheek felt rough under her fingertips. He hadn't shaved since yesterday, and she couldn't help but remember the feel of his beard against her own skin, on her lips and her breasts, her stomach—

She dropped her hand away. Thoughts like that would only increase the desolation in her heart. "Your friend, Mike, did you reach him this morning?"

"Yes. He'd dug a little deeper in the computer, and he confirmed that Howard had altered your files and established a phony business number under the name Phillips. If we hadn't discovered it, Victor could have changed everything back and no one would have ever known."

"You mean after he had me." A shiver ran up her spine.

There was a rustle in the bush outside the cave. Caleb went rigid, then placed his hand to her mouth, listening. The bush shook, along with the chatter of a squirrel and a disagreeing blue jay. Caleb relaxed and slowly removed his hand.

Sarah released the breath she'd been holding. "And Mike?" she whispered. "What was he going to do with me?"

"We were supposed to meet someone outside of town." He moved away from her, farther into the darkness of the cave. "Obviously that plan's been changed. Once I've picked up a few things here, I'll have to take you in myself."

Picked up a few things here? Confused, Sarah listened to him fumble in the darkness. She heard the snap of several metal buttons, then the rasp of a zipper. The beam of a flashlight suddenly lit the back wall of the cave. Caleb knelt in front of a large knapsack. She moved closer and watched him sort through the objects inside. Her throat went dry.

Guns.

Not just ordinary guns. Big, black rifles with strange attachments, smaller, silver revolvers with long, menacing barrels. Sophisticated, high tech weapons that weren't intended for hunting animals. At least, not the four-legged variety, she realized with bone-chilling certainty. There were knives and what looked like explosives, too. A radio, clothes, some cans of food. It looked as if he was ready to ward off an invasion.

Or start one.

At the sound of Sarah's soft gasp, Caleb shone the light on her. He'd been so focused on what he needed to do he hadn't fully considered the impact it might have on her to view his "emergency kit," his ace in the hole in case he'd ever been caught off guard away from the cabin.

"Caleb?" Her eyes were wide, her face ashen as she stared at the arsenal in front of him.

He set the flashlight down beside him and moved toward her, cursing silently when she flinched.

"Sarah, there are some things I haven't told you about what I do."

She glanced at the guns again. "You sell insurance."

"I'm not an insurance agent," he said quietly. "I'm a government agent."

"Government?" Her voice was barely audible, and even in the dim light he saw the sudden jump of fear in her eyes. He felt disgust for himself, for what he was and what he did.

"You're with the FBI, too?" she asked weakly.

He shook his head.

"CIA?"

"No."

"Oh, God, Caleb," she whispered hoarsely. "At least please tell me it's *our* government."

He couldn't help but smile at that. "Yes, but there are agencies that people don't know about, Sarah. Agencies that are known only to a very few high-level government officials."

"And you work for one of those?" she asked incredulously.

He nodded.

"And your friend, Mike?"

"He's my boss."

"Your boss? And just what exactly is it you do? No, never mind—" she shook her head and touched her temple with shaking fingers "—I'm sure you can't tell me, and I'm sure I really don't want to know."

He couldn't, and she wouldn't, of course, Caleb knew. As it was, he'd already told her more than she should know. More than was safe for her to know. And at this moment, there was nothing that concerned him more than her safety.

Handling Victor Howard and his men would be child's play if Sarah weren't involved. In fact, he would actually enjoy the encounter. But she *was* involved, and before he dealt with Howard, he had to make sure she was out of the way. He had to get her away from here, out of the mountains, then he'd deal with Victor.

As if to protect herself, she folded her arms and sank back on her knees. "What are you going to do with me?"

He felt a knot form in his gut at the way she stared at him. As if she'd never seen him before. He remembered the way she'd looked at him last night and this morning, as no other woman had ever looked at him before. That look had made him want things, and for just a little while, even one night, he'd almost wondered if it were possible.

But the look in Sarah's eyes, the fear, was his wakeup call. He could never have a life with her. With any woman. And he knew now that after Sarah there would never be another woman.

He grabbed a revolver and tucked it into the waistband of his jeans.

"I'm not going to do anything with you, Sarah," he said without emotion. "I'll get you out of here and deliver you to Mike. He'll take care of you from there."

In spite of the dim light, he saw a brightness in her eyes. She blinked several times and looked away. "All right."

The quiet hurt in her voice was like a vise around his chest. The sudden need to touch her, to hold her, overwhelmed him. He reached for her, then froze.

Someone was outside the cave.

# Nine

Caleb put up a hand, signaling silence. Sarah waited, breath held, then heard the sound of a man's voice close by.

"They had to come this way," a man said. Luther. "You search this area and I'll head north. Victor's gone to call for backup."

She heard the sound of boots scrambling over rocks, then a deep, angry mumbling. She realized it was Frank; he was close, nearly on top of them. He cursed repeatedly. The wild hammering of her own heart nearly drowned out the man's fervent complaining. Afraid to move, afraid to breathe, she waited until the footsteps faded.

Caleb moved quickly. He reached into the knapsack, then pressed a gun into her hand. She trembled at the feel of the weapon in her palm.

"Use this if you have to," he said grimly and moved toward the cave entrance. "Just make sure you don't shoot me when I get back."

Terror shot through her at the thought of being alone here. "Where are you going?"

A thin, tight smile lifted one corner of his mouth; his eyes shone like black fire. "A quick business meeting. I won't be long."

She touched his arm as he turned to leave. "Caleb...I..." She couldn't speak, her throat felt too tight. But if she couldn't tell him how she felt, then she would show him. She set the gun down and pulled him to her, wrapping her arms around his neck as she pressed her lips to his. His hands tightened on her arms, and she thought he might push her away. With a low, throaty groan his arms came around her, nearly crushing her as he deepened the kiss.

He ended the kiss abruptly, then looked at her long and hard, his face like granite. He reached into his back pocket and pulled out a business card and slipped it into her hand.

"If I don't come back in twenty minutes, get out of here. Head north until you come to an empty cabin, then break in and use the phone there. Call the number on this card and ask for Mike. You can trust him."

She nodded, then watched as he disappeared outside. He didn't look back.

Legs crossed, she sat and stared at the gun in her lap. She'd never even held a gun before, let alone shot one. Could she? She wouldn't know until faced with the situation. But she did know that if Caleb didn't come back, if anything happened to him, that she certainly would want to use it, not for herself, but for him.

She glanced at the knapsack lying two feet away from her and a cold shiver rippled through her.

*An agent.*

She closed her eyes, trying to absorb what Caleb had told her about himself, but her mind was still reeling. An agent. How could it be possible? She opened her eyes and looked down at the gun in her hands. The cold metal burned her fingers.

But it *had* been there all the time, she realized now. Everything about Caleb set him apart from other men. The way he held himself, the way his dark eyes were always watching, waiting, assessing. He was a man in control. Power and danger emanated from him.

What a naive little fool she was. How could she have ever believed that a man like Caleb sold insurance?

She understood now why he'd seemed so suspicious of her. If what he did was so secretive, so confidential, then no doubt he was trained not to trust anyone, not to let anyone close to him. Especially not some strange woman who claimed she had amnesia.

She jumped at the sound of a snapping twig directly outside the cave. How long had it been? She'd been so deep in thought she'd lost track of time. Her fingers tightened on the gun. Someone, or something, rustled the bushes.

Heart hammering, hand shaking, she pointed the gun at the cave entrance.

The bushes parted and the silhouette of a man blocked the light. Her finger tightened on the trigger.

"Hi, honey. I'm home."

*Caleb!* With a deep sigh of relief, she lowered the gun.

"I hope you don't mind," he said, moving into the cave, "but I brought some company."

Wolf bounded in behind Caleb. He leapt at her with a joyful whine, knocking her over. Laughing, she wrapped her arms around the huge animal and gave him a hug.

"Where did you find him?" she asked, tolerating a wet, sloppy kiss on her cheek from the happy wolf.

"He found me." Caleb rubbed Wolf's neck.

She ran her hands over the animal's thick fur. "Is he all right?"

"He's fine, which is more than I can say for our friend Frank. That man certainly has had a bad day."

Sarah watched Caleb move to the knapsack and flip on the flashlight again. A box of ammunition went into his jacket pocket, then a thick wad of money. A chill went through her when he slipped a small knife into his boot.

"Did you . . . I mean, is he . . ."

"I didn't kill him. I was tempted, but I decided it would be a lot more fun to let him wake up and remember the last thing he saw was my fist. I'd also love to see his expression when he figures out why he smells so bad."

"What do you mean?"

Caleb's grin was wicked. "Wolf happened along about then. I guess he figured the guy was in his territory."

Sarah's eyes widened. "He didn't!"

"'Fraid so."

She covered her mouth in horror, but couldn't stop the giggle that bubbled up.

Caleb crawled out of the cave, looked around, then reached in his hand and grinned at her. "So what do you say, Miss Grayson, shall we blow this joint?"

She needed no encouragement. She took his hand and followed him. They ran, with Wolf beside them, silently and swiftly, straight to the empty cabin he'd told her about. She waited anxiously while Caleb broke into the cabin, and when they couldn't find the keys for the pickup in the carport, she waited while he hot-wired the truck.

And as they headed out of the mountains on a rarely used back road, Sarah sat back in the seat and closed her eyes, recounting the events of the past twenty-four hours.

She'd regained her memory, made love for the first time, been kidnapped, chased and shot at. She'd also held a gun, broken into a house and stolen a car.

Amazing what a difference a day made.

At the sound of the shower water running, Caleb sat on the edge of the motel bed and picked up the phone. He dialed, then glanced at his watch. Five-thirty. That made it eight-thirty Washington time. Someone picked up after half a ring.

"Yeah?"

"Mike, it's me."

"Caleb! Where the hell are you?"

Caleb glanced at the notepad on the nightstand. The Palm Tree Motel. But he wasn't quite ready to give an exact location. Not even to Mike. "A motel in Los Angeles. Sorry I missed the pickup. We ran into a little problem."

"So I heard. My men said your place looked like a shooting gallery. You all right?"

"Yeah, I'm fine." He heard the shower door slide open, then close. "Look, Mike, I need a few things. You can get them faster than I can right now."

"I thought you wanted me to handle this."

"That was before. It's personal now."

There was a pause. "I see. What do you need?"

He told him. Mike had him hold while he checked availability. The shower went off as Mike came back to the phone.

"You can pick them up in two hours." Mike gave him the address.

Caleb hung up the phone, then pushed the drape aside and looked through the window of the room to the truck. He'd left Wolf in the front seat, and if anyone came near, Caleb would know immediately.

The drive back into the city had taken two hours, then they'd picked up a change of clothes and toiletries at a small department store, driven through a fast food restaurant and found this motel.

"I thought I heard you talking to someone."

Caleb turned. Sarah stood in the doorway, watching him while she towel dried her hair. She'd changed into a white, scoop-necked sweater and brown slacks. Just looking at her, coming out of the bathroom with her bare feet and flushed skin, made his throat go dry.

He dropped the curtain back into place.

"I had to let Mike know we were all right."

Her hand stilled. "When will they be here?"

He frowned at her. "Who?"

"The men." She stared at the towel in her hand. "The ones you were going to take me to this morning."

It seemed like a hundred years ago now. A lifetime. "They aren't coming."

She looked up at him. "They aren't?"

"No."

"But I thought—"

"I'm going to take care of it myself." He'd almost said take care of you, but he'd caught himself in time.

"Oh." Her eyes narrowed with confusion. "Why?"

He stood there, watching a drop of water as it slipped down her neck and into the neckline of her sweater. He wanted to touch her, to follow the path of that water drop with his lips and tongue. He clenched his jaw and looked at her. "You know why, Sarah."

She held his gaze for a long moment. "Yes."

"You also have to know that it doesn't change anything between us. As soon as I've taken care of Howard, I can't see you again."

"Because of what you do?"

The hurt in her eyes almost had him moving toward her. But she had to understand. He had to *make* her understand. "Because of what I do, because of who I am. There are dozens of men like Howard out there who would welcome a way to get to me, to find a weak spot. You would be my weak spot."

"I could live with that, Caleb."

He shook his head. "No, you couldn't live with it. That's my point. And I sure as hell couldn't let you, wouldn't let you."

She watched him for a long moment, then dropped the towel in her hand and moved toward him. "Such a strange way to tell me you care about me, Mr. Hunter."

The purpose in her stride and the determination in her eyes had him taking a step back. "It doesn't matter what I feel for you, Sarah. It doesn't matter what either one of us feels. It can't change anything."

She closed the space between them, then looked up at him and shook her head slowly. "But it does, Caleb. Maybe not for tomorrow, or the day after. But for now, for this moment, it matters more than you can possibly realize."

She touched his face, and her fingers were cool and smooth on his rough cheek. The feminine scent of her, fresh from the shower, with her skin damp and her hair wet gave her a sensuous, exciting look. He desperately wanted to touch her, to ease the ache building in him. How foolish of him to think he could have had one night with her and it would be enough. He knew now one night, one week or one year wouldn't be enough. A lifetime wouldn't be enough.

He kept his hands stiffly at his sides. He wouldn't touch her. He couldn't. He flinched when she traced the line of his jaw.

"Last night," she said softly, "when I thought that would be my one and only time with you, I thought I'd been given the most precious gift in the world. And now I've been given another gift, one that's even more precious." She lifted her gaze to his. "The courage to tell you that I love you."

A motorcycle roared by outside and somewhere, in another room, Caleb heard the drone of a television. But here, in this room, in this world with Sarah, there was only the sound of his heart pounding in his temples. Every denial, every argument that had been screaming in his brain suddenly went silent.

*I love you.*

He'd heard the words before, even said them. But there were no names and no faces that matched those words. There was only Sarah, with her pale blue eyes and soft silky hair. Sarah, with her quiet determination and pure heart. This morning she'd offered herself to Victor Howard in order to save him. His chest tightened at the thought of what might have happened.

"Sarah—"

She touched his lips with her fingers. "Don't say anything, Caleb. Please. I won't try to change your mind, or force myself into your life. I just want you to know."

She rose on her tiptoes and pressed her mouth to his. Blood raced through his body, and the feathery brush of her lips against his sent all rational thought from his mind.

He had to hold her, to feel her in his arms, to taste her again. He pulled her up against him and bent down to her, covering her mouth with his. She sighed deeply, and the warmth of her breath on his face burned him. Her lips parted, welcoming, eager, and she wrapped her arms around his neck, pulling her body closer to his. His kiss was long and deep, hungry, and the soft sound of pleasure from deep in her throat snapped the last thread of his control.

With a sound resembling a growl, Caleb lifted her off the floor, molding his body to hers. Her breasts pressed against his chest as he carried her to the bed. She held tightly on to him, pulling him with her as they sank to the mattress.

Her hair spilled around her face in a fury of damp curls. He positioned his body over hers, keeping his weight on his elbows as he kissed her again and again. Her hands moved hungrily over his chest, where she unbuttoned his shirt and slid the garment over his shoulders. Her fingertips on his hot skin inflamed him, and his body throbbed with the need to feel those hands everywhere.

Lifting his mouth from hers, he watched her passion-heavy eyes open slowly and look at him. She spoke to him silently with those eyes, holding his gaze as she ran her hands down his chest to the snap of his jeans. He sucked in a sharp breath at the touch of her knuckles against his stomach, and the agonizingly slow downward hiss of his zipper brought his senses to a fever pitch.

She gasped as he rolled suddenly onto his back, bringing her on top of him. Her sweater was off in one swift move and the front clasp of her bra open. She started to pull away from him, not realizing that she'd positioned herself exactly the way he wanted. He cupped her breasts with his hands, then covered one hardened peak with his mouth. She moaned, squirming against him as his tongue swirled hot and wet over the hardened tip, instinctively moving the juncture of her thighs against his arousal. Every soft whimper, every little moan, pushed him closer to the edge, until he thought he might go mad from wanting.

Mindless, Sarah rocked her body against Caleb's, increasing the ache that filled her body. His mouth and tongue on her breast sent exquisite ripples of pleasure through her, ripples that intensified and centered between her legs. She dragged her nails over his chest, then raked her fingers through his hair.

"I love you," she whispered without hesitation, without reserve.

He moaned, then suddenly she was on her back again. Caleb looked down at her, his dark eyes intense, his breathing ragged. She smiled and touched his cheek, then his lips. With his gaze holding hers, he took her hands in his, kissed each one, then lifted her arms over her head while he gently kissed her lips, her neck, her breasts. She tossed her head back and forth, frustrated that she couldn't touch him, and at the same time her excitement was heightened by his tender entrapment.

"Caleb, please," she cried, writhing under him.

He ignored her, just continued his slow torturous exploration of her body, finally releasing her hands as he moved lower. He slid her pants and underwear off in one liquid-smooth movement, then removed his own while he traced the valley of her hips with his mouth. And when he moved lower still, and his lips and tongue caressed the most intimate part of her, a pleasure unlike anything she could have possibly imagined consumed her. She heard the sound of her own voice sobbing his name, but she sounded far away. She twisted the bedspread in her fists, moving uncontrollably in a spasm of intense ecstasy.

His body rose over hers and he slid into her, catching the wave of her pleasure as he thrust deeply, her name on his lips ragged and hoarse. She clung to him, arching upward wildly as the wave crested. He shuddered powerfully, again and again, and when he finally stilled, she wrapped her arms around his neck and held him tight.

"I can't move."

Sarah's breathless announcement several moments later made Caleb smile. He pressed his lips to her neck, then each breast. She shivered at his touch and slid her fingers through his hair. He started to move, but she pulled him back.

"No," she whispered. "Don't move. Stay right where you are."

"Right where I am, huh?" he said teasingly.

She slowly opened her heavy eyelids and looked at him. The blue was deeper than he'd ever seen them before, the look sensuous. Her skin was damp and flushed.

"Exactly right where you are," she repeated with a slow smile.

"You'll have to give me a minute if you have something in mind."

Her eyes widened and she asked with sheer innocence, "Only a minute?"

He laughed and moved inside her, bringing forth a sigh from her parted lips.

She moved her hands up his shoulders, then down his chest. His skin was slick, and her fingernails raked lightly over him. "I don't know anything about you," she whispered.

He nuzzled her ear. "I wouldn't say that's completely true."

"You know—" her breath caught as his hand cupped her breast "—what I mean."

He sighed, took hold of her hips and quickly rolled onto his back, careful not to break the contact between them. She gasped, then smiled, obviously pleased with the freedom and control he'd just given her. He was just as pleased with the view. "And just what would you like to know about me?"

"You mean I can ask?"

"Of course you can ask. Whether I can answer you or not, though, will depend on what you ask."

Her expression grew thoughtful, then she said, "Is your real name Caleb Hunter?"

"No."

She seemed surprised. "It fits you, you know. I can't imagine you a Hubert or a Wendell."

"Thanks, I think."

She studied his face for a moment, then touched the jagged scar over his left eyebrow. "How did you get this?"

He hesitated. "An explosion."

Her eyes widened. "You were in an explosion? How did—" she stopped suddenly "—no, never mind. That's not the part of you I want to know about. Do you have family?"

He shook his head. "My mom died when I was seven, and my dad took off when I was nine. I had a kid sister, Carrie, she was only three when our dad left, but we were split up and sent to foster homes. I never saw her after that."

"You have a sister and you never tried to find her?"

"I tried just before I went into the service at eighteen, but had no luck. Later, after I went to work for the government, I could have found her, I had the resources, but I decided it was better this way, not knowing."

Her expression softened as she ran her index finger over his chin. "She would be a weak spot, as you so lovingly refer to people you care about."

He sighed. "I can't care about anyone, Sarah. I'd only end up hurting them."

But he did care, she knew. Whether he admitted it or not, he cared. About her, about his sister. No matter how hard he tried, he wasn't the cold, unfeeling person he wanted her to believe.

"People get hurt every day, Caleb," she said softly. "Bad things happen. What matters is how you spend the time you do have. *Who* you spend that time with."

"You don't understand," he said harshly. "I've seen it, Sarah. Another agent—he was a friend—we had a meeting, an exchange of information. I stood outside the car, the agent and his wife were in the front seat. She joked with me about fixing me up, invited me for dinner—'' he closed his eyes and drew in a breath ''—the car exploded. I was thrown twenty feet. There was nothing I could do.''

When he opened his eyes again, she saw the anguish there. ''Oh, Caleb, I'm so sorry.''

''He'd always said he wanted out of our department,'' Caleb said a dry laugh. ''That was about the only way to do it.''

Her own throat tightened and her heart ached for him, for the agent and his wife. And when he looked at her again she saw a determination, an absolute and unshakable resolve that left her cold.

He would never bring her into his life. Never.

This was all they'd have. These few hours. She'd deal with her own heartache later, but for now, for this little slice of time, she would cherish every minute they had.

She brought her fingers to his mouth and traced the firm outline of his lips. No more words, she thought, and when he took hold of her hand and nuzzled her palm, she felt the desire rise again. Closing her eyes, she drew in a long, slow breath.

''Caleb?'' she murmured. ''Can I ask you just one more question?''

He slid one hand over her hip and rear end. ''Hmm?''

''Exactly how many minutes does it take before you—''

Laughing, he pulled her to him and answered.

# Ten

It was dark when she woke. The heavy drapes were drawn, but yellow light from the motel sign flooded in from the sides, giving shape to the sparse furniture in the room. She heard a door slam from a neighboring room, then the roar of a car engine before it drove away. She stared at the illuminated dial on the night-stand clock. Eight-fifteen. She'd been asleep for almost two hours, since Caleb had left. He hadn't told her where he'd gone or when he'd be back, but he had left explicit instructions not to answer the door or phone.

Dragging her hands through her hair, she sat on the edge of the bed and tugged at the large white T-shirt Caleb had given her to wear. Wolf, who'd been sleeping on the floor beside her, greeted her with a wet tongue on her cheek.

"Hello to you, too," she said sleepily, rubbing the animal's head.

For the moment, at least, she felt safe here. Victor was probably still looking for them in the mountains, and even if he had realized that they'd managed to get away, there would be no way he could trace them here. No one had seen her face when they'd checked in, and just in case Victor had figured out they'd stolen the truck, Caleb had switched plates with another car parked in a long-term parking lot for the L.A. airport shuttle service.

She stretched lazily, then stared at the bathroom door, uncertain if she could make it that far. Her arms and legs were weak, her muscles sore. But the luxury of a hot bath gave her the strength to pull off her T-shirt and manage the few feet.

A few moments later, when she lowered herself into the steaming tub, complete with strawberry-scented bubbles from a complimentary motel bath gel, a long sigh escaped her. Closing her eyes, she leaned her head back against the cool porcelain, letting the heat from the water ease the aches in her body.

She smiled slowly, remembering in exquisite detail exactly why her body was so sore. She recalled every touch, every whisper, of making love with Caleb earlier. The masculine scent of his skin, the coarse, erotic texture of his hands on her body. In spite of the warm water, she shivered. Her skin felt tight and sensitive, and merely thinking about him brought waves of pleasure radiating through her. A little more than two hours had passed since they'd made love, and already she wanted him again.

There was so little time left, and that thought made her ache inside, with need, with longing. Because it was too painful, she refused to let herself think beyond the moment. Whether she had five minutes or five hours with Caleb, she would remember every precious second.

It felt as if she'd lived her entire life on Pause. After she'd lost her parents, Granny had sheltered her, and then after Granny had become ill, there'd been no time for herself outside of the library. Robert had been one of her few friends, and she was going to miss him. Victor Howard was going to pay for killing him, she thought angrily. She intended to make sure of that. Whatever it took to put the man away, she would do it.

After that, she knew that she would never see Caleb again, that she would go back to her life as it was before. No, not like it was before. Nothing would ever be like it was before. Not after Caleb.

At least he would know that she loved him. If nothing else, she'd given him that to take with him.

A wave of water suddenly splashed over her face. Gasping, she sat straight up. Caleb knelt by the tub, a frown on his face, but a smile in his eyes.

"First rule," he said, "is never close your eyes while taking a bath."

"You scared me half to death," she sputtered, wiping at her face.

"Nice bubbles."

She felt the heat of a blush on her cheeks as he stared at her wet body, his gaze lingering over her breasts. His eyes darkened suddenly and the smile was gone.

Biting her bottom lip, she sank back down under the water.

"You know what I've never done?" He stood slowly and began to unbutton his shirt.

She shook her head.

"Taken a bubble bath."

Her eyes widened as his hand went to his zipper. "Caleb, you can't, I mean you wouldn't..."

"Wouldn't what?"

Jeans and boots were gone. He stood naked in front of her. Beautifully, powerfully, naked. It was her turn to stare now.

"Fit," she said, her breath suddenly quick and shallow.

He smiled. "I fit very well," he said, his expression intense as he lowered himself into the tub. In one easy move, he sat and pulled her on top of him. Water splashed over the rim.

Gasping, Sarah fell forward, hands splayed on his wide chest. He circled her waist with his hands, positioning her body, then with a sigh of intense pleasure, he entered her.

Waves of heat shimmered through her. He cupped her breasts with his large hands, and she closed her eyes.

"What did I tell you," he said, his voice harsh and strained, "about closing your eyes when you take a bath?"

She smiled and opened them again, holding his dark, fierce gaze with her own. She took him deeper inside her, saw his eyes narrow and his jaw tighten as she moved sensuously over him. His hands moved to her buttocks and held tight as he drove himself upward with long, hard strokes. Sarah moved with him, amazed that the need could rise so quickly and with such urgency. The scent of strawberries enclosed them;

bubbles burst and floated in the air. Water sluiced over their bodies and splashed over the sides.

Her fingers curled into his chest, and with a soft, strangled cry, she arched her back. The tension inside her shattered, and he gathered her close, crushing her to him as his own powerful release shuddered from his body into hers.

Still holding her, he leaned back, his breathing as ragged as her own. Water lapped at their skin, and the tiny popping sound of disintegrating bubbles surrounded them.

He kissed her, slowly and thoroughly. Gently. She cupped his face in her hands and savored the taste of him, the feel of his tongue mating with hers.

With a contented sigh she lay in his arms, her head nestled under his chin. Neither one of them cared that the water had long since cooled and the bubbles disappeared.

"I've brought you a present." Caleb's gaze followed the path of the towel he used to dry off Sarah's bare shoulders and back. Her skin was still flushed from their lovemaking, and she smelled like strawberries.

"Please tell me it's food." She leaned back against him while he wrapped the towel around her.

He smiled and kissed the curve of her neck. "Pizza," he said, then pulled on his jeans. "But that's not the present."

He took hold of her hand and pulled her back into the room. There were two three-foot-high stacks of newspapers sitting on the table with a pizza box on top. Confused, she simply looked at him.

"A little reading material." He sat her on the bed, grabbed the pizza, then stretched out on the bed beside her, resisting the temptation to tug at the knot holding together the towel she wore. "Hope you like peppers and pineapple."

"Doesn't everyone?" She picked the pineapples off a slice and dropped them on a piece Caleb went for. "Why do I need reading material?"

Wolf rose from the spot he'd adopted by the door and came over to investigate the smell of food. Caleb reached into a bag and pulled out a bowl and a small box of dry food.

"Robert had written something," he said, setting a bowl of food in front of the animal. "Something that Victor hadn't wanted him to write about. We've got to figure out what it was."

She stared at the papers with disbelief. "Robert wrote entertainment editorials for two newspapers, plus free-lance articles for the arts and leisure section of the *Times*. Where and how could you possibly have come up with all of those articles in a couple of hours?"

He shrugged. "I don't have them all. Just the past six weeks before his death. I'm counting on what we're looking for being in one of those."

She sighed heavily and reached for the T-shirt she'd left lying on the bed. "Six weeks or six years. How will we know what it is that we're looking for?"

He watched with interest as she discarded the towel and pulled on the T-shirt, fascinated by the way the cloth molded itself to her damp breasts. With a rueful sigh, he tossed a handful of papers at her, then settled back with a stack for himself and another piece of pizza. "I'm hoping we'll know when we see it."

"And if we don't?" she asked quietly.

He saw the fear in her eyes, the unasked question. "It's here. I know it is. We'll find whatever button it was that Robert pushed, and we'll nail Victor's butt."

"Can't you just have him arrested?" she asked. "He killed Robert and tried to kill me."

Caleb shook his head. "Even Mike can't have an FBI agent brought in without some kind of proof. Right now it's your word against his. There would have to be an investigation, which would give Howard time to cover his tracks."

"And get rid of me," she added.

He slid across the bed and pulled her into his arms. "He won't get close to you again," he said softly. "I won't let him."

She laid her head against his chest and ran her fingers lightly over his arm. "I'm so sorry I brought you into this. I couldn't live with it if anything happened to you."

It amazed him how the slightest touch from her aroused him, not only physically, but deeper, in a place where no woman had ever been before. Where no woman ever would be again. He needed her to be safe, even though it meant that once she was, he would never see her again.

"I'm not sorry," he murmured. "And nothing is going to happen to me."

She pulled away, her gaze piercing as she searched his face. "Is that a promise?"

He'd never made a promise in his life. He didn't believe in them. Didn't trust them. But looking at Sarah, watching the blue of her eyes deepen as she looked at him, he would have promised her anything. "I promise."

There was a sudden passion in her eyes he'd never seen before, an intensity that shone like fire in blue ice. "See that you keep that promise, Hunter," she said tightly, then shoved a newspaper at him. "Start reading."

Four hours, three dozen book reviews, fourteen theater openings and countless museum showings later, they were no closer than before they'd started.

Caleb sat sprawled on the floor at the side of the bed; she sat at the table, squinting at the blurred print in front of her. She'd read the same sentence three times and still didn't know what it said.

With a groan, she arched her back and glanced at the clock. One-thirty a.m. Except for a short break where Caleb had taken Wolf for a walk and settled him in the truck cab for the night, they hadn't stopped.

"You okay?" Caleb asked without looking up from the newspaper spread across his knees.

"Wonderful," she said crossly, and immediately regretted her tone. Caleb had been tireless, forcing her to drink some of the coffee he'd brought back with him and gently waking her every time she'd fallen asleep, teasing her that he shouldn't have kept her up the night before. She reminded him that she'd done her fair share of keeping him up, as well.

Setting his paper aside, he rose and walked over to her, stepping over his "maybe" pile, which Sarah was to reread after she'd finished her own. "Why don't you go on to bed," he urged gently.

She shook her head. "I only have three more papers to go through, then the stack you've set aside for me."

He leaned over her and glanced at the article she was reading. "What's this one?"

Stifling a yawn, she rolled her head to loosen the knot that had crept into her neck. "Robert did a series of articles about a group of ten paintings by a seventeenth century artist named Mouton, which were stolen twenty years ago." She frowned at the black ink on her hands, then wiped it off on a napkin. "A few months ago seven of those paintings were discovered in a warehouse in Los Angeles. Robert was very excited about the finding and wrote an entire article on each painting. I'm working my way backward. This is number three out of seven, a piece titled *Carnal Interlude*."

"I'd like to see that one," he murmured, brushing his lips over her ear.

It didn't seem possible that the need could still rise in her as quickly as before. But it did, and she shivered at his touch. "You're too late," she whispered. "They're going to be auctioned off next week, privately. Unless, of course, you have twenty or thirty million stashed away somewhere."

"That might take me a few days."

Not sure if he was kidding, she glanced up sharply. He grinned.

"What about you?" she asked, gesturing to his stack of papers. "Any possibilites?"

"There's a review on a mystery book about art forgeries. Robert slammed the book, stating, and I quote, 'Justice Department files were more interesting reading.' If Victor hadn't killed Robert, no doubt the author would have."

Sarah sighed. "Robert was a frustrated writer himself. He'd always wanted to write the great American novel about the art world, but was too insecure to actually start a book. He just did a lot of research.''

Caleb frowned. ''Did you ever help him?''

She shook her head. ''Never with the book research. He was very guarded about that, but I often downloaded bulletin board information and files for him from the International Foundation for Art Research and gathered data bases for artwork appearing on the international auction blocks. Nothing unusual, considering his work.''

''Didn't you say he used the computers at the library himself?''

''Of course. He even used mine occasionally, after hours, but we don't archive users' files. The user is responsible to keep his own disk. Everything connected to the main terminals is automatically deleted once a week. I cleaned everything out the day before I was supposed to leave for Mexico.''

''And you're sure he didn't leave any disks at the library?''

She pressed her fingers to her closed eyes. ''Yes, I'm sure. There weren't any at his office, either. He had no family, so one of the women in his office brought me the personal items from his desk. There was nothing unusual, certainly nothing suspicious. If he had any disks anywhere, Victor got there first and found them.''

''Not necessarily,'' Caleb said. ''That's what Victor's worried about. That Robert left something incriminating with you.''

''But he didn't,'' she protested. ''I don't know anything.''

"Maybe you do, and you just aren't aware of it yet," he said thoughtfully. "We'll work more on that in a few hours, after you get some sleep."

"I can't—"

"No arguments." He took her by the arm and pulled her to the bed. "We're both going to get some rest."

"Bully." She fell onto the bed with him and didn't resist when he pulled her to him. She snuggled against his shoulder. "You smell fruity."

He frowned sharply at her.

Smiling, she ran her lips over his neck, touching the tip of her tongue to his skin. "Strawberries," she murmured.

"That's what I get for taking a bubble bath," he muttered, and slid his hand under the back of her T-shirt.

"That wasn't all you got," she teased boldly.

He lifted his brows in mock surprise. "Why, Miss Grayson, you shock me. Whatever would the patrons of the library think if they heard such talk?"

Her lips moved over him like a hot whisper, tasting, exploring. "They'd say I was one lucky librarian."

Chuckling, he pulled her on top of him, inching her T-shirt up until bare breasts met bare chest.

"I thought you wanted to sleep," she breathed, moving down his chest. Her hands moved between them as she reached for the snap on his jeans.

He closed his eyes. "I am sleeping."

"So you're a somnambulist."

He didn't answer her for a moment, just sucked in a sharp breath as her lips traveled over his stomach. "A what?" he finally managed.

"You know, a sleepwalker." She slowly drew down the zipper on his jeans.

"I wouldn't call this walking," he said hoarsely, twisting his fingers in her hair.

"What would you call it?" she asked, then laughed softly at his crude response. The muscles in his stomach jumped and tightened as she caressed him with her mouth. The hard, velvety strength of him excited her, gave her courage to explore a sensuality she'd never dreamed existed in her.

With no thoughts other than of him and the newfound power of complete love, she moved over him, stoking the fire until it raged through them both, out of control. Nothing, and no one, existed out of this moment but the two of them.

Afterward, nestled in each other's arms, they slept.

*She stood at the edge of a cliff, surrounded by darkness. Snakes slithered out of the night, rising up in giant twisting coils, circling her... she tried to run, but her legs refused to move... relief poured through her as Caleb stepped forward between the writhing snakes, his hand outstretched. She reached for him, but it was no longer Caleb, it was Victor Howard. He laughed as she opened her mouth to scream. No sound came out. "M'lady," he said, his black eyes malevolent as his icy hand closed over hers, "I'm waiting for you...."*

Heart pounding, Sarah sat abruptly. She struggled to breathe; her hands shook as she dragged her fingers through her hair.

A dream. Thank God. Only a dream.

She released a slow breath, letting the nightmare fade and her fear subside. It seemed so real. Shivering, she clutched the covers to her naked body and reached for Caleb.

He was gone.

She called his name softly, thinking he might be in the bathroom. Silence. The clock glowed 4:30. Slipping out of bed, she parted the drapes and looked out into the parking lot. The truck was gone, and Wolf, too. When she turned on the light over the table, she saw the note he'd left: "Didn't want to wake you. Had to meet a fax coming in from Washington at five, our time. Expect to be back by seven. Bringing more newspapers."

She groaned aloud at that. She still had three more to read, plus the pile Caleb had set aside for her. Reluctantly she decided she might as well get them out of the way now.

A cool shower woke her up and she dressed quickly, pulling on the slacks and sweater Caleb had bought for her the day before. With a heavy sigh she sat on the bed and picked up where she'd left off, which was with the opening review for the showing of the recovered Mouton paintings. Robert started the article with a description of the painting: "Seduction whispered in her midnight eyes, passion flowered in her supple body, a flower waiting to be picked..."

Sarah read on, amused by Robert's interpretation of the painting. "But alas, this painting, *Silent Maiden,* along with *Portrait of a Mistress*, and *Lady in Waiting*, are three ladies that shall be kept waiting until the Gods of Art see fit to bring their abductor to justice..."

A slow, almost numbing sensation settled into her limbs. She stared at the words, but they blurred together and another image came to her... no, not an image, a voice. Victor's voice.

*My ladies are waiting for me.*

Those were the words he'd used that night in the mountains, when he'd been speaking to the other men. She'd mentioned it to Caleb when she'd regained her memory, but she'd assumed Victor had been referring to real women, not paintings.

Her heart started to beat heavily. Victor had stolen the paintings. That had to be it. Robert found out somehow, probably in his research, and when Victor found out that Robert knew, he killed him. She shook at the injustice of it, furious that vile, greedy men like Howard could so easily take the life of another.

But there was no proof. No evidence. Nothing to link Victor to the theft. He could easily fence the stolen work and, except for a bank in Switzerland, who would ever know?

But Robert knew. Using the library computers, he'd uncovered something, and she'd have to find out what it was. The files in the main computer would have been deleted, but there was a possibility that the steps he'd taken, the path he'd used, might still be in her own personal computer. If she could retrieve his steps, she'd be able to pull up the files and connect the dots.

It was a long shot, but it was the only shot she had.

She glanced at the clock. She needed to get into the library before it opened, while there was no one there. She didn't have her keys, but the guard knew her well; he'd let her in. She could download everything quickly and bring it all back here. She could even be back before Caleb returned, but just in case, she quickly scribbled a note as she called for a cab.

Victor Howard was going to jail, she told herself resolutely. And she intended to make sure he stayed there.

# Eleven

The office was small. Large enough for a desk, two file cabinets, a copy and fax machine and a computer. There were no pictures on the walls, no comfortable chairs. One window with bulletproof glass overlooked the now empty parking lot of the business center, and a complicated alarm panel inside and outside the entry door ensured total security, as well as complete privacy.

Caleb leaned back and stretched; the desk chair creaked and groaned under the pressure. With a heavy sigh, he downed the last of his coffee, then stared blankly at the piles of paperwork on the desk top in front of him.

Victor Howard, forty-four. Special agent, Federal Bureau of Investigation, twenty years. Worked in Law Enforcement Assistance, Justice Department and Internal Affairs. He'd reached a commendable security level, as Mike had already told him, but had received promotions slowly. Based on the files Caleb had received over the fax, it appeared they'd often been given reluctantly.

Twenty years. The man could retire any time he wanted. Why would he jeopardize his career and pension at this point by killing Robert and trying to kill Sarah? It had to be something big, and undoubtedly money was the motivator. Whatever it was, Robert had found out about it, Victor had killed him and had been cleaning up loose ends with Sarah when he'd brought her up into the mountains. It could have been weeks before anyone had found her body, which was obviously what Victor had been counting on. A flat tire, and Wolf, were the only things that had saved her life.

He thought of her that night when he'd found her, half-drowned, nearly frozen, and his rage at Victor rose to the surface. He crumpled the paper coffee cup in his fist and threw it into the trash can, his jaw tight and eyes narrowed with anger. He looked forward to his next meeting with Victor Howard.

Sarah had been sound asleep when he'd slipped out of bed almost two hours ago. She hadn't even stirred when he'd turned on the bathroom light to find his clothes. After he'd dressed, he'd stood over her, watching the rise and fall of her steady breathing, the soft curve of her fingers against her cheek. So innocent in sleep, he thought. Yet only a short time earlier, when they'd made love, *innocent* would have been the farthest word from his mind.

How could he ever have thought she was an agent? Too many years of mistrusting people, of watching over his shoulder, had left him with nothing and no one to believe in. He'd fought hard to hold on to that belief, but somehow, with her soft blue eyes and trusting spirit, she'd slipped in under his thick skin and into his heart. Nothing in his life had ever been more difficult than to admit to himself that he loved her.

He did love her. It still amazed him. And the only thing more difficult would be letting her go.

A new and different rage filled him. A rage at having to walk away from the only woman he'd ever truly cared about, the only woman he'd ever loved. A woman he would die for, not because she was his job, but because she was his next breath, his next heartbeat, his life and his soul.

And the fact that she'd been willing to die for him yesterday, that she'd offered herself to Victor to protect him, had left him shaken and overcome with an emotion he'd never realized he was capable of.

If only there was a way...

But there wasn't. The rage in him disintegrated and left a black, empty hole in its place. Agents didn't leave his department, and there was no way in hell he'd ever bring her into that life.

The fax machine sprang to life again, spitting out a response to the request he'd made for a listing of Victor Howard's assignments for the past five years. Caleb glanced over the report, which started with the present and worked backward. Victor's current assignment, which he was in charge of, dealt with surveillance of an insurance company employee suspected of transporting stolen art out of state.

Caleb straightened. Not for a second did he believe it was a coincidence that Howard's assignment dealt with art. He quickly scanned the earlier assignments, his gaze halting abruptly when one name nearly jumped off the page at him.

*Mouton.*

Cursing, Caleb grabbed the files, shut down the office and headed back to the motel.

The night guard at the library not only let Sarah inside, he loaned her the money for the cab when she explained she'd accidentally left her purse at home. After listening to the elderly guard's lecture on young girls being out at odd hours, she took the stairs to the third level, then entered the double doors that led to the fine arts department. When the doors closed behind her with a loud echo, leaving her in darkness, she felt as if the bottom of her stomach had dropped out.

She hadn't much time. It was nearly five-thirty. She moved past the main light switch, thinking it best if no one besides the guard saw her. The cleaning crew would be in sometime around six, and she wanted to get in and get out before they arrived.

Swallowing the lump in her throat, she felt her way through the rows of tall bookshelves and headed for her office at the back of the cavernous room. She'd worked enough late hours to know her way in the dark, and a moment later she sat at her computer and switched it on. The motor hummed and danced, then the screen glowed, filling the small room with a pale amber light.

She knew whatever documents Robert had worked on wouldn't come up automatically, but if his instructions to the computer still existed, she could at least follow the same path he'd taken through the Internet and find them. She pulled up his user ID number, entered the code, then sat back and watched the addresses appear. The Art Loss Recovery... International Foundation for Art Research...

The Justice Department.

Excitement twisted in her stomach. If her guess was right, she now knew what she was looking for: Mouton.

After a simple word search, she began to download everything in the files connected to the painter and the stolen pieces, plus descriptions of paintings, inquiries and private auctions.

She scanned the first few pages already printed out, stopping occasionally to absorb not only the information, but the implications. And as the pieces fell into place and she began to understand what Robert had stumbled onto, a chill seeped through her clear down to her bones. She had to get this information to Caleb, quickly.

She glanced at the clock on the wall. The second hand sprinted in circles while the printer strolled leisurely.

Hurry... hurry... *hurry*...

Fifteen minutes later she gathered the papers she'd printed and stuffed them into a folder. She reached for the Exit button on the computer.

"Hello, Sarah."

Her hand froze. Slowly she stood, then turned. The silhouette of a man filled the office door. He stepped into the room, and the yellow light from the computer screen glowed with sickening transparency on his unsmiling face. *Oh, God, no.*

Victor Howard.

"How did you get in here?" she whispered hoarsely.

"It wasn't difficult to convince the guard."

Panic rose in her, and she prayed they hadn't killed the man. Behind Victor, back in the shadows, she spotted another figure. Luther. No doubt Frank was close by, as well. There was no one she could call to. No one who could help. *Caleb, I'm so sorry. If only I'd waited.*

"How did you find me?" she whispered, pressing back against the desk.

"I admit we did lose you for a little while, but we assumed you'd return here at some point. Your friend, Mr. Hunter, is quite resourceful for a man who sells insurance. Something tells me there's more to his dossier than meets the eye." He sighed. "Given the time constraint, though, I'm afraid I won't be able to explore the matter before I—" He glanced at the folder in her hands and lifted his brows. "And what have we here?"

*Stay calm, stay calm . . .* "It's over, Victor. The police will be here any minute. They know what you've done."

He regarded her for a moment. "And what exactly is it they know?"

"That you were the agent in charge when the Mouton paintings were recovered in that warehouse in Los Angeles. That you only reported seven of the paintings found, when in fact all ten were there. It was you who stole the other three."

He shortened the distance between them with the same casual yet deadly approach a cat used on a bird.

"Federal agents are sworn to uphold the law of the country," he said with a sneer. "How could I violate a trust as sacred as that?"

"Maybe for the twelve million dollars a private collector in Germany was going to pay you for them."

She had to keep talking, to buy some time. "Robert found out through the Art Loss Register that the three Mouton paintings weren't listed as stolen, which meant that anyone could sell them quietly on the international market and no one would ever know.

"But Robert knew," she went on, gauging the distance between her and the door. Even if she made it past Victor, Luther was waiting only a few feet away. "He'd had a special interest in the Mouton paintings, so he'd dug deeper, asked questions. And everything led him to you. You found out and killed him."

"An interesting story." Victor reached into his pocket and pulled out a gun. "What a shame for you no one will ever hear it."

"I told you the police know." She stared at the gun, watched in horror as he screwed a long metal nozzle onto the barrel.

Victor sighed. "You're a terrible liar, Sarah. You wouldn't have gone to the police until you had proof. And I want to thank you for gathering that proof up for me in such a neat package. Makes it so much easier to dispose of and sweep clean any tracks."

"You'll never get away with this," she said, hating the quaver in her voice.

"Of course, I will. The cabdriver who brought you here was eager to cooperate with the FBI. I've already sent a man over to take care of Mr. Hunter at your motel." He smiled and glanced over his shoulder at Luther. "And as for you. Well, a young woman, working alone, raped and murdered. Happens all the time."

*Caleb!* God, no! Panic raced through her. He wouldn't be expecting anyone. She had to warn him.

But how? Victor was going to kill her right here, and then Luther would—

Her knees felt weak and her stomach turned at the thought. She looked at Victor's face, it glowed like an eerie yellow mask. Glancing at the monitor beside her, she realized the only light in the room came from the lit screen. The computer plugged in under the desk, right by her feet.

It was a long shot, but the only shot she had.

Clutching the file to her in one hand, she sank to her knees. "Please don't kill me," she cried, holding Victor's attention while she blindly reached under the desk for the outlet. "Please, I won't tell anyone, I won't. I'll do whatever you say. Anything."

She felt the cord and followed it. She continued to sob, then reached out in one swift move and jerked the cord out of the wall.

The room went dark.

Victor swore and she felt him move at her, but she lurched sideways and jumped up. She heard Luther yell as she ran through the doorway, then the crash as a chair overturned directly in front of her.

Still holding the file, she swerved to the right and felt her way down the aisle between two tall bookshelves.

"Find the light switch," she heard Victor yell furiously. "Just don't let her get away."

It was happening all over again. Just like that first night. Her heart pounded in her temples. She wouldn't let him win, wouldn't let him hurt Caleb. Dear Lord, where was Caleb now? she wondered. What if she were already too late to help him? She forced the horrible thought from her mind, refused to accept that possibility. She had to stay calm, to think.

She had the advantage of knowing every inch of the library. There were ten long rows of bookshelves, with an aisle dividing them, then several tables and chairs by the exit doors. She'd have to make her way through the maze of bookshelves, then to the exit. But she knew Luther or Victor would be waiting there, with Frank somewhere outside. She'd never make it past all of them. The only other exit was in the opposite corner, and that one led to the history section, which would take her even farther away from help.

Needing her hands free, she shoved the file behind a row of books. Luther and Victor were yelling to each other, and she heard the sound of books falling on the aisle next to her. She hadn't much time before Luther found the main light switch just inside the doors.

"Sarah," Victor hissed her name, and she knew he was close. Too close. "You know you can't get away. Don't make this so difficult."

Breath held, she felt her way to the end of the row, then picked up a light hardbound book and heaved it over the top of the bookshelf as far away from her as she could. It landed with a loud thud, and she heard footsteps running away from her. She removed her flats, tucked them under her arm and quickly moved through the rows of books, feeling her way until she reached the bookshelf closest to the history exit.

Victor and Luther were still yelling, searching for the light switch and for her. A few more feet, she told herself. If she made it through the doors, she could take the back stairs to the main level and call for help. The tile floor was smooth and cool on her bare feet.

She was almost there...

The light came on.

"Stop right there."

She stood in the open with no place to hide. Victor aimed his gun at her from across the room, his expression furious.

"Go get her," he snapped at Luther, who stood several feet away, his hand on the light switch by the entry doors.

An angry smile lifted one corner of Luther's mouth. His hand dropped from the switch as he took a step toward her.

The doors behind Luther burst open. With blinding speed a man lunged at Luther, knocking him to the floor, then swung on Victor, kicking the gun from his hand.

"Caleb!" Sarah cried out in relief, then screamed as Luther rose and came at Caleb with his fist raised. Caleb whirled and with one swift jab between Luther's eyes, sent the man crashing back to the floor, unconscious.

Victor stood facing Caleb, only now it was Caleb with a gun in his hand.

"Who the hell *are* you?" Victor asked, his eyes narrowed with rage.

Caleb smiled. "Just an insurance agent. Whole-life, term. Afraid you wouldn't qualify, though. After the courts are done with you, your life expectancy is going to be very short. You okay, Sarah?"

She wanted to run to him, to throw herself in his arms, but her legs weren't working properly, and all she could do was take a few shaky steps toward him. "Frank's still around here somewhere."

"Ah, yes. My buddy, Frank. I met up with him already, and we said hello."

"It was Victor who stole the paintings," Sarah said. "Robert found out and that's why Victor killed him."

"I know." Caleb kicked Victor's gun out of reach. "I did a little research of my own."

"So did we."

Sarah gasped at the sight of the tall, jean-clad man standing in the doorway. His hair was long and dark, his gaze intense as he moved into the room and took everything in. Two other men came in behind him and stood, waiting for instructions.

"Hey, Mike," Caleb said easily, "a little late, aren't you?"

"Looks like I timed it just right." The agent looked at Victor. "This our man?"

Victor glared at him. "I'm an FBI agent. You're interfering with a federal crime, and the penalty is—"

"Save it," Caleb cut him off. "Get this guy out of my sight, will you, Mike? I'm about to do something I'm sure I won't regret."

Mike motioned to the agents standing behind him. They moved toward Victor, but Luther suddenly leapt at Caleb, knocking him off balance. The agents went for Luther, leaving Victor alone. He dove for his gun lying a few feet away, then rolled and pointed it at Caleb.

Caleb jerked backward as the gun went off. Another shot rang out, this time from Mike's gun and Victor went limp.

Sarah screamed, watching helplessly as Caleb slumped to the floor.

The smell of antiseptic hung heavily in the hospital corridors, mingling with an occasional scent of roses that drifted from the nurses' station. An orderly dressed in blue studied a chart as he walked down the dimly lit hall, and Sarah watched anxiously as he passed through the double doors that led to surgery.

She'd tried several times in the past four hours to get through those doors, to talk to someone, anyone, who might tell her how Caleb was doing. Each time a guard on the other side had stopped her. Politely but firmly she'd been told there was no news and to wait. The nurses had been equally polite, as well as noninformative, and she hadn't seen Mike since he'd driven away in the ambulance with Caleb. One of the other agents had brought her here, then disappeared himself.

She was going crazy.

The nightmare repeated itself over and over in her mind. Victor aiming the gun...a sharp blast...Caleb falling...the sound of her own scream echoing over and over.

Victor was dead, and Caleb was lying on an operating table, fighting for his life.

It wasn't real. It couldn't be. After all they'd come through, everything that had happened. She refused to accept that he wasn't going to be all right. He had to be.

She couldn't lose him. Not this way. She couldn't stand it. She loved him too much to bear the thought of a world without him, even if his world didn't include her.

She straightened as a doctor came through the doors, her heart beating wildly as he moved toward her. But he walked past her to a couple waiting at the far end of the hall. She slumped back in her seat, blinking several times in an attempt to clear away the burning moisture.

She heard the sound of hushed voices and the quiet ring of a nearby phone. A cup of cold coffee sat on the seat beside her. The sight of it made her stomach turn.

She couldn't stand it anymore.

Swaying slightly, she stood and marched toward the double doors. When she pushed them open, the guard was there again, blocking her way. She met him, narrowing her eyes as she stared him down.

"You're either going to have to shoot me or arrest me," she said, her voice controlled and remarkably calm. "But I'm coming through and I'm not leaving until someone talks to me."

He started to argue, but she brushed past him, shoving him off when he reached for her arm. She started down the inner corridor and walked into the first room. It was empty. She made her way to the next room, ignoring the guard on her heels. A janitor was mopping the floor.

She moved toward the third room just as the doors opened and Mike stepped out. She saw a team of doctors inside, their masks off, looking at a chart. They glanced up when they saw her.

"Miss Grayson—"

"I'm going in," she said coldly.

He took hold of her arms. "Sarah—"

"Dammit—" She shook him off and swiped at the tears that suddenly spilled over. "*You can't stop me.*"

"Sarah," he said more gently, taking hold of her again. "I'm sorry."

Cold terror welled up inside her. She stared at him, trying to form words that wouldn't come.

Hesitating, he glanced over his shoulder to the room behind him, then looked back at her. His jaw was like granite, his mouth a hard, straight line.

"He's gone, Sarah," he said quietly. "And I am sorry."

Everything went black.

# Twelve

Wolf paced, his massive head raised high, his ears alert to the drone of a lawn mower next door and the laughter of children playing ball on the sidewalk outside. A breeze lifted the curtain from Sarah's open living room window, bringing with it the scent of freshly mowed grass and frying bacon.

*Life goes on,* she thought dimly and stared blankly at the cup of tea in her hand. People still slept and ate and mowed their lawns. Children still played. But there was no color anymore, no clarity or coherence. Every second, every minute, was like sand sifting through her fingers.

It hardly seemed possible that three weeks had passed. Time no longer had relevance. The sun came up, it went down. It got dark, it got light. Either way, it made no difference at all. Even the luggage that she'd packed for her trip to Mexico still sat in the middle of her living room. She might unpack, she might not. It simply didn't matter one way or the other.

She hadn't even been allowed to go to the funeral. Security precautions, Mike had told her. He also told her that he would be in touch with her again, but he hadn't. She'd called the number that Caleb had given her that day in the cave, but it was disconnected. She'd called six different federal agencies and no one had ever heard of a Mike Townsend. She'd seen a small article in the newspaper about the recovery of the three Mouton paintings, but there had been nothing about an FBI agent named Victor Howard, nothing about a shooting at the library.

It was as if none of it had ever happened. If it wasn't for Wolf, she would think she'd dreamed the entire thing. She closed her eyes and let out a long shaky breath.

But it wasn't a dream. It was real. Too damn real. And so was the pain that ripped her apart and left her open and raw.

But there was another reality. One that promised hope and gave her strength to go on.

She was pregnant.

Smiling softly, she slid her hand over her flat stomach. Her fingers tingled at the energy she felt radiate from within her. A baby. She was going to have Caleb's baby.

Tears blurred her vision, a mixture of pain and happiness. Pain for the fact that he would never know, never see his son or daughter; happiness that she still had a part of him with her. A part of him that she would always love and cherish.

She wasn't worried about being a single parent. She was fortunate that Granny had left a trust fund for her, so money wasn't a problem. And after what she'd faced with Victor Howard, nothing would ever frighten her again. Caleb had taught her to be strong, to fight. She would teach that to their child, though something told her that with Caleb being the father, strength and bravery and honor would be inherent.

Setting her tea down, she rose and moved into the bedroom, dressing carefully for her doctor's appointment. She wanted to look nice today, had even bought a new blue floral dress that she knew Caleb would have liked. He would be with her today in her heart, in her soul. He always would be.

She'd just finished combing her hair when she heard Wolf growl. At the sound of her doorbell, the animal started to bark furiously. Slipping on her shoes, she took hold of Wolf's collar and opened the door.

There were two of them. Dressed in dark suits, dark sunglasses. She didn't know their names, but she knew who they were. What they were.

Agents.

Her heart started to beat wildly. She took a long, slow breath, refusing to let herself be upset.

The shorter one with clipped blond hair showed her his badge and identified himself and his partner. Agent Walters and Agent Forster.

"Miss Grayson," Agent Walters said. "We would appreciate it if you would come with us. There's a matter pending that requires your attention."

Hysteria bubbled up inside her. *A matter pending?* She'd lost the only man she would ever love, and they were concerned about a matter pending? She seriously considered letting go of Wolf's collar, but years of etiquette won over her raging emotions.

"Agent Walters," she said, her voice tight and cold. "Four weeks ago three agents showed up at my door, asked me to go somewhere with them and then tried to kill me. Give me one good reason I should go with you now."

He shifted uncomfortably, then glanced over at the blue sedan parked in front of the house. She watched as the darkened back seat window slowly slid down.

It was Mike.

Tears burned the back of her throat. Mike was her only tie to Caleb. The only man who could tell her anything about her child's father. The one man whom Caleb trusted.

She pulled Wolf back inside and grabbed her purse. "I'll be back, boy." She gave the animal a hug. "You take care of things here."

She slid into the back seat with Mike and stared at him for a long hard moment. "You look amazingly real for a man who doesn't exist."

"What do you mean?" He signaled for Agent Walters to drive. Agent Forster walked toward another car parked in front of the house next door.

"I tried to call. No one's ever heard of you."

"We've had to do some reorganization. I'm sorry it's taken me so long to get back to you."

"If you tell me you're sorry one more time," she said, her voice barely controlled, "I swear I'm going to hit you."

He looked at her with surprise, then nodded. "Okay."

"Where are we going?" she asked as the car moved onto the freeway.

"Someplace safe we can talk," he said. "It's not far from here."

"I've heard that song before."

"I understand how you feel, Sarah. You have every right not to trust me."

"You have no idea how I feel," she whispered, then blinked back the tears.

"You're right," he said quietly. "And I'd apologize, but I'd rather you didn't hit me."

She smiled weakly, but there was no more conversation. They drove for maybe thirty minutes then got off the freeway and headed into an industrial center in the middle of the San Fernando Valley. A small, private airport lay beyond the warehouse where Agent Walters parked the car.

A Cessna roared by overhead as Mike opened the car door for her.

"Inside here," he yelled over the noise and pointed to the warehouse.

There were two four-passenger planes inside the building and a series of offices in the back. Mike took her arm and led her into the first office. Pictures of airplanes decorated the wood-paneled walls. Mike pointed to one of the two chairs across from a large wooden desk. "Why don't you sit?"

Arms folded, she faced him. "I want some questions answered, Mike. You owe me that much."

"I owe you a lot more than that," he said sincerely. "But you really need to sit."

She shook her head. "I don't want to sit. I want you to talk to me. Please."

"I think you better sit, Sarah."

Sarah froze at the sound of the familiar voice behind her. *Dear God, it can't be . . . it can't be . . .*

Her heart hammered against her ribs. Breath held, she turned slowly.

Caleb.

The room started to spin. Mike grabbed her as her knees gave out. Caleb moved beside her, taking her in his arms. Gently he set her on the chair.

"I'll come back in a little while," Mike said, closing the door behind him.

Caleb. It really was him.

She stared at him, but she couldn't speak. He was alive. Wonderfully, beautifully, incredibly alive. She smelled the spicy scent of his after-shave, felt the rough skin of his hands on hers as he knelt beside her.

Her fingers shook as she touched his freshly shaved cheek. "You're not dead."

He smiled slowly. "No, Sarah. I'm not."

"But, how . . . what—"

He cut her words off with his mouth, kissing her deeply, passionately. She clung to him, still afraid to believe it was true, that he was real. Afraid that he was a dream inside the nightmare she'd been living.

He pulled her tightly against him until she slid off the chair and onto the floor with him. They knelt, torso to torso, her arms wound around his neck, her breasts pressed against his strong wide chest. She kissed him back, letting him feel what words could never say.

She cupped his face in her hands, then slid them down between them, needing to feel his body. Her fingers grazed the bandage under his shirt, and she pulled away breathlessly.

"Victor shot you," she whispered, lightly touching the bandage.

Nodding, he covered her hand with his. She gloried in the feel of his heartbeat under her fingers.

"The bullet passed through me without hitting anything vital. I'll have some recovery time, but I'll be fine."

Caleb watched the play of emotions that raced across Sarah's face. Disbelief, relief, and the one he'd been most afraid he wouldn't see: love. Her eyes and skin glowed as she looked at him. He saw everything there, everything he'd ever want and could ever hope to have.

She pulled away suddenly, her expression fierce. "You lied to me."

"Not exactly." Caleb winced under the heat of her accusal. "Mike told you I was gone, which was true. As soon as the surgery was finished, I was transferred to a private hospital. That's where I've been."

She wasn't to be appeased so easily. "All this time you've let me think you dead. Have you any idea the hell I've been in for three weeks?"

"I'm sorry, Sarah, I—"

"If one more person says that to me, I'm going to shoot them myself."

He smiled, but knew enough not to push the issue. "I was drugged pretty heavily the first few days, and when I managed to come out of it enough to ask Mike about you, he told me he'd given you the impression I'd died."

Fire danced in her eyes. "He more than gave me—"

He brushed his lips against hers, not only to silence her, but because he had to touch her, to taste her. "You're right. But he was doing what he had to do. He had to get me out of there, quietly, without anyone knowing. He also had to keep the Victor Howard incident quiet, not only because I became involved, but because the FBI wanted to handle the situation themselves."

Tears filled her eyes. "I thought you were dead, Caleb," she said, her voice trembling. "I wanted to die, too."

He pulled her into his arms, let her cry against his shoulder. After a few moments she quieted, and he pressed his lips to her temple.

"When I was on the surgery table, before they put me out completely, all I thought about was you, that if I died I'd never see you again. And yet I knew I could never see you again even if I lived. I wouldn't risk your life." He tucked a loose strand of her silky hair behind her ear. "When I came to and was coherent enough to understand that Mike had told you I'd died, I knew it was my chance, my only chance to ever live a normal life."

She pulled away from him, her brow furrowed. "What chance?"

"To stay dead," he said softly. "To everyone but you and Mike, of course. He was the one person who could arrange it. It took some convincing, but he finally gave in." He took her by the shoulders and looked down at her. "Caleb Hunter is dead, Sarah. But this man, the man who loves you, who wants to marry you, is alive."

She stared back at him, and as his words finally sank in, her lips parted and her eyes widened. With a cry of joy, she threw herself into his arms and hugged him, then quickly let go. "Oh! Did I hurt you? Oh, Caleb—" she stopped. "I don't even know what to call you now."

Grinning, he pulled an ID card out of his pocket and handed it to her. She read it and her gaze jerked back to his.

"Hubert Wendell Holmes!"

He shrugged. "You called me Mr. Holmes once, and told me I didn't look like a Hubert or a Wendell. Unfortunately those were the first names that came to mind when Mike asked me who I wanted to be. Think you can live with it?"

"Can I live with it? I can't live without it, without you." Needing to touch him, to remind herself he was alive and it wasn't a dream, she cupped his face in her hands. "And what about me? Do I have to change my name, too?"

"I was planning on taking care of that," he said. "How does Mrs. Sarah Holmes sound?"

He grinned, and she touched the creases beside his mouth. "It sounds wonderful, but there's another name I'm going to have to get used to, as well."

He kissed her, having a hard time himself believing that she was really his. "And what's that?"

She pressed her lips to his. "Mommy."

He went very still, then slowly pulled away from her.

"In about eight months," she said, her eyes shining.

Stunned, he simply stared at her. A baby? She was having a baby? His baby?

He hauled her into his arms, crushing her to him, unconcerned about his wound. And when he kissed her, he wasn't sure if the salty tears he tasted were Sarah's or his.

"I assume that means you're happy," she said breathlessly when he finally let her go.

He swore softly when a knock at the door interrupted them. Mike stuck his head in, raising one brow at the sight of them on the floor. "There's someone here who'd like to see you, if you have a minute."

Caleb frowned, then laughed when Wolf bounded through the door and nearly leapt on top of him, barking and yipping. Both he and Sarah succumbed to the animal's wet kisses before Caleb commanded him down.

"Forster said there was luggage already packed, so he brought that, too," Mike said, then closed the door again.

Caleb looked at her questioningly. "Were you going somewhere?"

She shook her head. "They were still packed from the trip to Mexico I never took."

He thought about that for a moment. "I don't suppose that little bikini is in one of those bags?"

She smiled. "It is. But if you expect me to wear it, it will have to be soon. A beach ball will have more shape than me in a few months."

He pressed his hand to her stomach as if he might feel the life growing there. He couldn't stop smiling. "I love you," he said and kissed her gently.

"And I love you."

The words filled him. For the first time in his life, he felt whole, complete. "Where would you like to live?"

"In a cabin, in a cave," she said, then meshed her fingers with his. "Wherever you live."

Wolf barked and they both laughed. "And you, too, Wolf," she added.

Wolf lay down and placed his head flat between his front paws, watching his master and mistress share a kiss.

"I think he's lonely," Sarah whispered when Wolf whined.

"Hmm." Caleb glanced at the forlorn animal. "You think he should have a mate, Mrs. Holmes?"

Sarah smiled and curled her arms around Caleb. "No one should be alone. Don't you agree, Mr. Holmes?"

"Absolutely, Mrs. Holmes," he murmured and lowered his lips to hers. "No one."

*     *     *     *     *

**SILHOUETTE®**

*Desire*

He's tough enough to capture your heart,
Tender enough to cradle a newborn baby
And sexy enough to satisfy your wildest fantasies....

He's Silhouette Desire's MAN OF THE MONTH!

From the moment he meets the woman of his
dreams to the time the handsome hunk says *I do*...

Fall in love with these incredible men:

In July:         *THE COWBOY AND THE KID*
                 by Anne McAllister

In August:       *DON'T FENCE ME IN*
                 by Kathleen Korbel

In September:    *TALLCHIEF'S BRIDE*
                 by Cait London

In October:      *THE TEXAS BLUE NORTHER*
                 by Lass Small

In November:     *STRYKER'S WIFE*
                 by Dixie Browning

In December:     *CHRISTMAS PAST*
                 by Joan Hohl

**MAN OF THE MONTH...ONLY FROM
SILHOUETTE DESIRE**

# Take 4 bestselling love stories FREE

## Plus get a FREE surprise gift!

The spirit of the holidays...
The magic of romance...
They both come together in

HOLIDAY HONEYMOONS

You're invited as Merline Lovelace and Carole Buck—
two of your favorite authors from two of your favorite
lines—capture your hearts with five joyous love stories
celebrating the excitement that happens when you
combine holidays and weddings!

Beginning in October, watch for

**HALLOWEEN HONEYMOON** by Merline Lovelace
(Desire #1030, 10/96)

**Thanksgiving—**
**WRONG BRIDE, RIGHT GROOM** by Merline Lovelace
(Desire #1037, 11/96)

**Christmas—**
**A BRIDE FOR SAINT NICK** by Carole Buck
(Intimate Moments #752, 12/96)

**New Year's Day—**
**RESOLVED TO (RE)MARRY** by Carole Buck
(Desire #1049, 1/97)

**Valentine's Day—**
**THE 14TH...AND FOREVER** by Merline Lovelace
(Intimate Moments #764, 2/97)

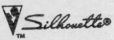

Silhouette®
TM

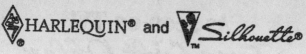

are proud to present...

# HERE COME THE GROOMS™

Four marriage-minded stories written by top Harlequin and Silhouette authors!

Next month, you'll find:

| | |
|---|---|
| *The Bridal Price* | by Barbara Boswell |
| *Annie in the Morning* | by Curtiss Ann Matlock |
| *September Morning* | by Diana Palmer |
| *Outback Nights* | by Emilie Richards |

**ADDED BONUS!** In every edition of
*Here Come the Grooms* you'll find $5.00 worth
of coupons good for Harlequin and Silhouette
products.

On sale at your favorite Harlequin and Silhouette
retail outlet.

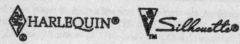

# As seen on TV!
## *Free Gift Offer*

With a Free Gift proof-of-purchase from any Silhouette® book,
you can receive a beautiful cubic zirconia pendant.

This gorgeous marquise-shaped stone is a genuine cubic
zirconia—accented by an 18" gold tone necklace.

(Approximate retail value $19.95)

# Send for yours today...
## compliments of ▼ *Silhouette*®

To receive your free gift, a cubic zirconia pendant, send us one original proof-of-
purchase, photocopies not accepted, from the back of any Silhouette Romance™,
Silhouette Desire®, Silhouette Special Edition®, Silhouette Intimate Moments®
or Silhouette Yours Truly™ title available in August, September or October at your favorite
retail outlet, together with the Free Gift Certificate, plus a check or money order for
$1.65 U.S./$2.15 CAN. (do not send cash) to cover postage and handling, payable
to Silhouette Free Gift Offer. We will send you the specified gift. Allow 6 to 8 weeks for
delivery. Offer good until October 31, 1996 or while quantities last. Offer valid in the
U.S. and Canada only.

## *Free Gift Certificate*

Name: _____

Address: _____

City: _____ State/Province: _____ Zip/Postal Code: _____

Mail this certificate, one proof-of-purchase and a check or money order for postage
and handling to: SILHOUETTE FREE GIFT OFFER 1996. In the U.S.: 3010 Walden
Avenue, P.O. Box 9077, Buffalo NY 14269-9077. In Canada: P.O. Box 613, Fort Erie,
Ontario L2Z 5X3.

---

## FREE GIFT OFFER
ONE PROOF-OF-PURCHASE

084-KMD

To collect your fabulous FREE GIFT, a cubic zirconia pendant, you must include this
original proof-of-purchase for each gift with the properly completed Free Gift Certificate.

084-KMD

Continuing in October from Silhouette Books...

This exciting new cross-line continuity series unites five of your favorite authors as they weave five connected novels about love, marriage—and Daddy's unexpected need for a baby carriage!

You loved

*THE BABY NOTION* by Dixie Browning
(Desire 7/96)

*BABY IN A BASKET* by Helen R. Myers
(Romance 8/96)

*MARRIED...WITH TWINS!* by Jennifer Mikels
(Special Edition 9/96)

And the romance in New Hope, Texas, continues with:

*HOW TO HOOK A HUSBAND (AND A BABY)*
by Carolyn Zane (Yours Truly 10/96)

She vowed to get hitched by her thirtieth birthday. But plain-Jane Wendy Wilcox didn't have a clue how to catch herself a husband—until Travis, her sexy neighbor, offered to teach her what a man really wants in a wife....

And look for the thrilling conclusion to the series in:

*DISCOVERED: DADDY*
by Marilyn Pappano (Intimate Moments 11/96)

DADDY KNOWS LAST continues each month...
only in Silhouette®

# You're About to Become a

# *Privileged Woman*

**Reap the rewards of fabulous free gifts and benefits with proofs-of-purchase from Silhouette and Harlequin books**

# Pages & Privileges™

It's our way of thanking you for buying our books at your favorite retail stores.

**PROOF OF PURCHASE**
SD-PP180
Offer expires October 31, 1996

**Harlequin and Silhouette—the most privileged readers in the world!**

For more information about Harlequin and Silhouette's PAGES & PRIVILEGES program call the Pages & Privileges Benefits Desk: 1-503-794-2499

*Silhouette*®

SD-PP180